FIGHTING FOR THEIR LIVES

Jacqueline Drunasky

ISBN 978-1-63874-564-8 (paperback)
ISBN 978-1-63874-565-5 (digital)

Christian Faith Publishing
832 Park Avenue
Meadville, PA 16335
www.christianfaithpublishing.com

Printed in the United States of America

To the doctors, nurses, paramedics, police officers, firefighters, all the people who have served and are serving. They keep our people in America safe. They sacrifice their lives every day so we can be safe, free, and healthy.

And to my daughter who inspired me to publish this very story, thank you.

CONTENTS

INTRODUCTION

This story is about a couple who are told they can't have any children. The miracle happens that they prayed for. Caroline gets pregnant. Seven months into the pregnancy, Caroline started to go into premature labor. She started hemorrhaging. She and the unborn child started fighting for their lives. The minute the baby was born, she had to fight to live. When the baby went home for the first time, the baby had a loving family. Five years later, Jeff, her father, got killed by a drunken driver. Kristen, the baby, grew up angry at the world. Caroline went into a depression and started drinking. She fell into the trap of the addiction to alcohol and not spending enough time with her daughter. Kristen's life from having a happy family turned into a dysfunctional family. Against all odds, will this family pull together and find happiness again?

Caroline and Jeff ran into each other at a college football game. Jeff was walking up to the hot dog stand when he saw Caroline. They started talking while waiting in line. Caroline was twenty-one years old, about five feet six tall and thin, and had long jet-black hair. She was going to school to become a social worker.

"Caroline, hi! How is your night going? Are you here alone?" asked Jeff.

"I'm doing all right, and yes, I am here alone, Jeff. How's it going for you?" Caroline said.

"Good, do you want to hang out with me? I promise I'll be a gentleman. Please, Caroline, give me a chance," said Jeff.

"I noticed you in high school, Jeff, but you never noticed me. It took you until now to notice me, but sure, I guess I can hang out with you," answered Caroline, grinning.

Jeff was six feet two tall with a husky build. He had sandy-blond hair cut short and was twenty-two years old. He was going to college to become a computer technician. Jeff and Caroline had two years left until graduation. They got along so well, and they became best friends and started dating.

During their last year of college, Jeff and Caroline got married. Two years after graduating, they wanted to have a baby and decided to start a family. Two more years went by, but still there was no baby. They went to the doctor's office to see what was going on. The doctor ran some tests on them. When the test results came back, there was bad news.

Caroline couldn't have a baby because her eggs weren't fertile. Jeff was very understanding. He told her it was up to God, not the doctor, whether she would ever have a baby. They kept trying for another year until Caroline became discouraged. They finally gave up trying to have a baby. At least they would always have each other.

Six months later, Caroline started feeling nauseous. She was always tired and began having fainting spells. Jeff started to worry about her. She was his soul mate. If she got sick, he could lose her. Just thinking about losing her made his heart feel like it was being torn out of his body. Jeff had to persuade Caroline to go to the doctor's office.

"Caroline, something is wrong with you. I think you should go see a doctor, honey. I love you so much, and I don't want anything bad to happen to you, please," Jeff begged.

"Jeff, I agree something is wrong. I have not been feeling like myself lately. I feel sick to my stomach all the time. I am so glad that I have a husband who cares so much about me that he notices important things. I'll go to the clinic tomorrow, Jeff," Caroline replied.

The next morning, Jeff got up early to make breakfast for Caroline so she wouldn't have to do anything before she went to the clinic. Before Jeff made breakfast, he went to the grocery store to get a rose for Caroline.

When he returned, Jeff made Caroline two eggs, bacon, and toast. He put them on a tray with a glass of orange juice and a glass of milk. After Jeff put the food on the tray, he placed the rose on the tray and went to the bedroom to wake Caroline. He carefully put the tray on top of the old antique dresser, leaned on the bed next to Caroline, and gave her a kiss on her cheek.

"Honey, wake up, my gorgeous queen! It's time for you to eat your breakfast that the cook downstairs made for you! Wake up," Jeff whispered in her ear. Suddenly, her eyes popped open, and she had a smile on her face.

"You didn't, did you?" Caroline looked over at the dresser and saw the tray. "Oh! You did make me breakfast. You're the love of my life! Thank you, Jeff."

Before she could finish talking, the tray was next to her. Jeff gave her another kiss on the cheek, and then he went downstairs to eat breakfast because his food was getting cold.

Twenty minutes later, Caroline came downstairs. Jeff was sitting at the table reading the newspaper. Caroline put her arms around his neck and said, "I love you, Mr. Winters, and don't you ever forget it!"

"I love you, Mrs. Winters, and don't you ever forget it! Now hurry, we have to go to the clinic. I talked to my boss, and he told me I could have today off. I can go to the clinic with you. I wouldn't have it any other way. I'm your husband, and I want to be there with you." Jeff smiled at her and got up. He walked over to the closet next to the front door, opened the door, and grabbed Caroline's violet and pink jacket and his navy blue jacket. Jeff walked over to Caroline and gave her the jacket. They put their jackets on and walked out the front door and headed for the clinic.

Jeff and Caroline got to the clinic just on time. They sat for a few minutes. Then the nurse called her name (Caroline). Jeff watched her go through the sliding doors. He waited and waited until he fell asleep.

Forty-five minutes later, Caroline came out to the waiting area and saw Jeff sleeping like a baby. She went up to Jeff and nudged him.

"Jeff, wake up. I've got some good news."

Jeff opened his eyes, and Caroline said, "Jeff, we're going to have a baby, another addition to the family!" Jeff's eyes got so big it looked like they were going to fall out. He started tearing. He was so happy. He felt like he was on cloud nine.

"Caroline, are you positive? Are we really going to have a baby? God is giving us the miracle we've been praying for. How many weeks?"

Caroline cut Jeff off and said, "I'm three months pregnant, but the doctor says I have to take it easy, or I could lose the baby. The doctor says I am at high risk of losing our baby."

"Don't worry, honey, we won't lose the baby. You are going to take it easy. I'll do everything. You'll do very little, and the baby will be just fine. Let's go home so you can rest. I don't want you overdoing anything. I want you to stay off your feet as much as possible." Caroline went to the doctor regularly to make sure the baby was all right, but in her seventh month, she started to have trouble. She was having pains. She began to worry, so she called the clinic to set up an appointment to see the doctor.

That night, while Jeff and Caroline were eating supper, her water broke, and she started to go into labor. Minutes after Caroline's water broke, she began bleeding. Jeff saw the blood on her dress, and he ran to the phone to dial 911. He dropped the phone when he heard Caroline fall to the kitchen floor. Jeff ran to Caroline, who was lying on the floor unconscious. Tears started to run down his cheek. "Caroline, don't worry, the ambulance is on its way. Just hang on, honey. Please, God, don't let her or the baby die." Shortly after he had called 911, a police officer had arrived at the scene. He was a young rookie, and he had a tall and thin build to him. It seemed like it took forever while he was waiting for the ambulance, but it was only ten minutes. Jeff was so worried that he rode in the ambulance with Caroline. On the way to the hospital, the baby's heartbeat started to drop. The paramedics yelled at the driver to hurry, or they could lose them both. Tension was in the air.

"She's going into premature labor, and she's hemorrhaging. Are we almost to the hospital?" the paramedic asked the driver.

"Yes, we're a mile away!" answered the driver.

The paramedics were very frustrated. Finally, they arrived at the hospital. A doctor rushed out the emergency door, ran to the ambulance, opened the door, and jumped in. He looked at Caroline, felt her stomach, and took her pulse. Then he checked the baby's heartbeat. He told the paramedics to get her in the hospital. He yelled, "Tell the nurse to get her prepped for surgery. I'll meet them in the operating room." He looked at Jeff and said, "Mr. Winters, we need you to sign some consent forms. We have to do a cesarean section, or your baby will die. Your wife is hemorrhaging. Both your wife and the baby could die. I'll send the nurse out with the papers immediately. I have to go." The doctor ran into the hospital. Jeff stood next to the ambulance stunned. It was like the whole world was caving in.

Finally coming back to reality, Jeff walked into the hospital. The nurse, in her midthirties, was already waiting for him. When he came in, she handed him some papers and pointed at the spots where he was to sign. After Jeff signed the papers, the nurse said, "Hi!

My name is Judy. Your wife will be okay, Mr. Winters. She's in good hands. One of our best doctors is doing the surgery. All you can do is wait now. As soon as I hear something, I'll let you know. Follow me. I'll show you where the waiting room is. Jeff followed the nurse to the waiting room and sat down on a chair next to the television.

"Mr. Winters, can I get you something to drink while you're waiting?" asked the nurse.

"I guess some coffee would be nice. I drink it black with a teaspoon of sugar. Thank you for being so nice to me. How long will this surgery take?"

"It could take four hours more or less. I don't know because it varies from patient to patient. I'll have your coffee in a few minutes." A couple of minutes later, the nurse came back with the coffee and put it on the table next to Jeff's chair. "Mr. Winters, I'll let you know something when I know something." Jeff drank the coffee and tried to relax, but he couldn't. It was too quiet, so he turned on the television.

Three hours later, Judy came into the room. "Jeff, you have a beautiful baby girl, but she isn't breathing on her own. Her little lungs are not yet fully developed, so she's hooked up to a respirator and a heart monitor. She weighs four pounds and three ounces. She's very weak and little, but she is really feisty. She surely can cry louder for not having developed lungs. Your wife is still being worked on. When I left, they had stopped the hemorrhaging and were closing her up. I would say in forty-five minutes, they should be done. Within an hour, you should be able to see her. You could go and see the baby now if you would like. I'll take you to the nursery."

Jeff got up and followed the nurse. When they got to the nursery, Judy, the nurse, handed him a long robe, scrub pants, scrub shirt, shoe covers, gloves, a cap, and a face mask to put on. The nurse showed him where he could change. Jeff changed, and then he and the nurse went into the nursery. The nurse took him to the baby who was in an incubator.

Judy explained, "Your baby is in the incubator and is hooked up to a respirator because her lungs are not developed all the way. We have to keep all germs from getting to her. She is susceptible to pneumonia. She'll be hooked up to the respirator until her lungs are fully developed. Have you and your wife discussed what you were going to name your baby?"

"Yes, we are going to name her Kristen," answered Jeff.

"Kristen is a beautiful name. Well, Kristen is quite a fighter," Judy commented.

Judy walked away to get a sticker to write Kristen's name on it to put on the incubator. Jeff stared at Kristen, amazed at how she was sleeping with all the tubes hooked up to her. Kristen was very tiny. Her hair was jet black like Caroline's, and the color of her skin was a dark pink, almost red. You could see blue veins through her skin, and she looked so helpless. Jeff started tearing again, wondering if his little girl would survive. He started talking to Kristen, "Hey, my little Half-pint, you keep fighting for your life. You have everything to live for. Your mommy and daddy love you so much. You're our little miracle baby. Don't give up now, Kristen. You've come so far already. Mommy will see you when she is feeling better. For now, you'll have to settle for second best, me, your daddy. Half-pint, we waited a long time to have you. I won't give you to anyone, not even to the angels. They'll have to take me before they get you. I'll have to pray to God so they won't try to take you. God blessed us with you, Half-pint. I know you probably don't understand what I'm saying. That's okay, Half-pint, anything for you!"

Kristen turned her face where her dad was standing. Slowly she opened her bright, blue eyes, looked at him, then closed them again. Judy came back to check on Kristen and put the sticker on the incubator. She looked at Jeff and said, "Mr. Winters, looks like your little girl is curious about you. You're going to be a good father. I see it in you. She is going to have everything she needs."

"Can I come back when you feed her and watch?" asked Jeff.

"You sure can. I'll even come and get you if you want. Your wife is in room 144 down the hall. She is still sleeping, but you can go in there to see her and wait until she wakes up," said Judy.

"Are you going to bring my wife to the nursery later, so she can see our new addition to the family?" asked Jeff.

"Yes, we are going to bring your wife to the nursery so she can see Kristen, your new addition to the family," answered Judy. Judy had a grin on her face and almost burst out laughing. She had never heard anyone put it that way before.

Jeff smiled and started to leave to go see his wife. Before he did, he looked at Kristen and said, "See you later, Half-pint. I'll see you with Mommy. Be strong. I love you, Half-pint."

After leaving the nursery, Jeff went to the gift shop and bought two bouquets of flowers. One was a rose bouquet with six beautiful white roses, baby's breath, and two ferns. The other was a carnation bouquet with soft pink carnations, three yellow poms, and two ferns. Then Jeff went to Caroline's room. He looked at her, then asked the short, hefty nurse tending to Caroline if she could put the two bouquets into vases. The nurse took the bouquets from him and left the room. Five minutes later, she returned with two vases containing the flowers. She put the flowers on the nightstand next to Caroline's bed and left the room so Jeff could have some privacy. Jeff sat in the chair next to Caroline's bed. Fifteen minutes later, Caroline began to awaken.

"Wake up, my gorgeous queen. Our little princess has arrived. She's a fighter like her mom," Jeff said.

Caroline looked at her husband. He had a big grin on his face of happiness. Caroline saw a twinkle in his eyes. Caroline started smiling, and tears rolled down her cheeks.

"We have a little girl? Is she okay? Can I see our little Kristen?" she asked.

"Later, my queen, you have to rest for a while, and so does our little princess. The nurse is going to take you to see Kristen, our little Half-pint, later. Rest, honey, so you are up to seeing her."

Caroline started to laugh. But it hurt where the stitches were, so she stopped. She agreed with Jeff that she should be well rested to see their little princess. Caroline closed her eyes. Then she started to drift off. Jeff waited until Caroline fell asleep, then left the room to call his boss.

After calling his boss, Jeff went back into Caroline's room. He sat in the chair next to his wife's bed. He fell asleep quickly, not having gotten much sleep the night before. Three hours later, Jeff woke up. Caroline was still sleeping. Judy came into the room to see if Caroline had awakened.

"Your wife is still sleeping? Maybe I should come back later?" asked Judy.

"No, Caroline should be waking up soon. It's okay, please wait," answered Jeff.

"Okay, we are going to feed Kristen shortly. I talked to the doctor, and he said it would be okay." Judy waited until Caroline woke. She helped Caroline get out into the wheelchair and took her to the nursery window.

"Oh, our little princess. She is so tiny and so beautiful, Jeff!" said Caroline.

"Kristen is as beautiful as her mother! She is as strong as you too. Caroline, you and Kristen are going to be here in the hospital for quite a while," said Jeff.

Jeff and Caroline admired their new baby. Judy went into the nursery to feed Kristen. Jeff and Caroline looked through the glass and watched as Judy fed Kristen.

Suddenly Kristen's heart rate started to drop. Judy quickly pushed the incubator into the room next to the nursery and yelled for a doctor.

Jeff and Caroline stared at each other, listening to what was happening in the room. Caroline became upset and started screaming for Kristen. She tried to get out of the wheelchair, but Jeff grabbed her and tried to hold her down so she wouldn't hurt herself. He yelled for a nurse hoping someone would come to help him.

"Caroline, stop. You're not going to help our little girl by endangering your recovery. Please, our little girl is a fighter. She needs you to get better, honey."

One of the nurses came running out. She saw Jeff struggling to keep Caroline from getting out of the wheelchair. Quickly she ran into the room where the doctor was working on Kristen. The doctor told her to sedate Caroline and that he was too busy trying to save the baby.

The nurse went to the supply cart containing the pills and vials. She grabbed a needle package, tore it open, grabbed a vial, and stuck the needle in it. After she filled it, she ran into the hall where Jeff struggled to keep his wife from getting out of the wheelchair. The nurse quickly gave Caroline the shot. Caroline fell unconscious.

"Are my wife and baby going to be all right?" asked Jeff

"Mr. Winters, I hope your wife's stitches didn't come out. Thank you for restraining her until I could do something. I tried to get here as fast as I could. Your wife should be fine, but if this happens again, it could hurt her recovery." The nurse looked at Caroline's stitches and noted they weren't pulled out.

"What about Kristen? You didn't say anything about our baby," said Jeff.

"I'm sorry, I don't know how your baby is. The doctor is still working on her. I really am sorry. He will be out to check on your wife when he can. I have to go."

The nurse went into the room where the doctor worked on Kristen. Jeff felt numb and dazed at what had just happened. He stood next to Caroline who was still unconscious in the wheelchair. Jeff watched through the glass and stared at the door to the room where Kristen was. He waited ten minutes until Judy came out to talk to him.

"Mr. Winters, your baby is in critical condition. The doctor is going to move her to the intensive care unit on the third floor. It looks like she is stable but not out of the woods yet. We want to be prepared in case something happens again. Your little girl doesn't want to give up. They'll be watching Kristen around the clock in the intensive care unit," Judy explained.

"Is Kristen going to live, or could I lose her?" asked Jeff.

"Right now, we're not sure. That's all we can tell you. The only thing I can say is pray as much as you can," said Judy.

Judy took Caroline to her room. Jeff walked with her. After she put Caroline into bed, Judy walked to the elevator. Jeff followed her to the intensive care unit. Judy gave him scrubs to put on. After Jeff changed, he went in to see Kristen. He stood next to the incubator where his almost lifeless little baby was fighting for her life.

"Hi, my little Half-pint. I told you I would come back to see you later. Here I am. You gave us quite a scare, Half-pint. It is really rough right now for you, but if you don't give up, it will get easier for you. Eventually you will be going home with Mommy and me," said Jeff.

Jeff stood staring at Kristen. He remembered the day he found out Caroline was pregnant. How happy he was about the joy that he felt inside. Jeff had a smile on his face. Reality hit him again. He didn't realize how complicated it could get. Jeff looked at Kristen, lifted his hand up, and touched the side of the incubator by her head. Slowly Kristen opened her eyes and stared at her daddy.

One week later, Caroline was doing better, so her doctor signed papers so she could go home. There was no change in Kristen though her condition was stable; she was still in critical.

Caroline and Jeff visited her every day, staying for hours at a time. They took turns reading stories to Kristen and talked to her encouraging her to keep fighting to get better.

The second week, Kristen's condition started improving, but she was still in the hospital for weeks. Each day, she got stronger and stronger. Kristen was not sleeping as much. Her eyes were open. She was responding more, and she was aware of what was around her.

Whenever Jeff and Caroline were there to visit, she smiled. When Kristen's lungs were developed, the doctor took her off the respirator. She was breathing on her own. The nurses and doctors were attached to Kristen. She had a lot of visitors because the nurses and doctors came to see her on their breaks. They called her the miracle baby. Kristen started gaining more weight. She was making a steady recovery, so the doctors took her out of the intensive care unit. She was no longer in an incubator. She was in the nursery with all the other babies. To be on the safe side, the doctors kept the heart monitor on Kristen for a few more days.

Weeks went by, and Kristen had gained two pounds. She now weighed six pounds, three ounces. It was time for her to go home. Jeff and Caroline were so happy when the hospital called them that morning and told them they could take Kristen home. They both rushed to get dressed, made breakfast, ate, and quickly did the dishes. Then they grabbed their jackets and headed to the hospital.

When they arrived, they went straight to the nursery. Before reaching the door, three nurses and two doctors came out of the nursery. Jeff and Caroline looked at each other and worried that something might be wrong with Kristen. The nurses and doctors looked sad. Jeff broke the silence and asked, "Is something wrong with our little Kristen? Did something happen before we got here?"

"No, Mr. Winters, we just hate to see Kristen leave. We all have grown attached to your little girl. It kind of makes us sad. We're going to miss our little 'miracle baby.' That's all. We've been visiting her practically every day. You and Mrs. Winters have such a special, miracle baby. We came to see her one more time before you took her home. Thank you for letting us visit her," said one of the doctors.

Jeff looked at Caroline, who had a big smile on her face. He shook their hands and said, "Thank you all for taking such good care of our little girl. She would never have survived if it weren't for all of you. Thank you again."

They were all grinning as they walked down the hall. Caroline and Jeff watched them as they went around the corner. Judy came into the hall with Kristen in her arms. She had a big smile on her face.

"Here is your little Half-pint, Mr. and Mrs. Winters. Kristen must know she's going home with you. She has had this smile on her face since she woke up," said Judy. She put Kristen in Caroline's arms. Caroline was so happy; tears rolled down her cheeks. Judy handed Jeff a bag with diapers, books on how to care for babies, and other stuff. Judy told Jeff and Caroline to wait while she ran into the nursery and grabbed a teddy bear and the chain bracelet that all the staff members chipped in to buy for Kristen. The teddy bear was white with red paws. On its tummy was a heart. In the middle of the heart, it read, "Our Little Miracle Baby." The chain bracelet had a scripture on it that read, "May the angels protect our little miracle baby." Judy handed Jeff the teddy bear and put the bracelet on Kristen's wrist. Jeff looked at Judy who had tears in her eyes.

"Thank you so much for helping me and my wife through the times when we didn't know for sure if Kristen was going to pull through. You helped us a lot from day one. When my wife was brought here, you showed me where to go and went out of your way to do things for us. This hospital is very lucky to have good, caring people who have a lot of patience. Judy, please tell everybody thank you for getting Kristen the teddy bear and the bracelet," said Jeff.

"Well, honey, should we take our little Half-pint home?" asked Jeff.

"Yes, it has been too long for us to be separated from our little girl," answered Caroline.

They said goodbye to Judy and walked down the hall. Caroline walked with her head up high. She was so proud to have such a special baby. Kristen was covered with a soft, pink, cotton blanket. They left the hospital and headed home.

Time passed, and Kristen grew quickly. Jeff and Caroline took her for checkups every month until she was two years old. After Kristen turned two, the doctors only needed to see her every three months. Jeff and Caroline loved Kristen unconditionally. Once a week, they took her to the zoo and then to McDonald's so she could play with other children on the playground.

Not a day went by without Jeff and Caroline realizing how lucky they were to have Kristen. Years passed, and Kristen was now five years old and playing like a normal child. If a person were to look at her, he or she would never believe the baby was a preemie. This particular Saturday morning, Kristen was watching cartoons in the living room when she heard the phone ring. Jeff and Caroline were in the kitchen talking. Jeff answered the phone. He talked for a few minutes and then hung up. Jeff went upstairs to get ready for work. Caroline started to wash dishes. He gave Caroline a hug and a kiss and said, "Honey, my boss needs me to come to work. We have a few computers down. They need me to fix them. Okay? When I get home from work, we'll take Kristen to the zoo. I love you, my gorgeous queen. I will see you later, my love." Jeff went into the living room where Kristen was watching cartoons and said, "Kristen, my little Half-pint, I have to go to work and fix some computers. I have some presents that I picked up yesterday after work for you and your mother. Don't tell Mommy, okay? I want to surprise her when I get home. This is just between you and me, Half-pint, okay? We'll go to the zoo after I get home too. Well, Half-pint, I'm going to be late for work if I don't leave now. How about a hug for Daddy?"

Kristen gave him a hug and said, "Daddy, I love you. Is Mommy staying with me?"

"Yes, sweetie, Mommy is staying home with you. I love you too, Half-pint. Take care of Mommy while I am gone," said Jeff.

Kristen watched her dad pick up his briefcase. As he turned the doorknob, then he opened the door, Jeff turned around and looked at Kristen and said, "See ya later, Half-pint!" and waved goodbye. Kristen waved goodbye back as he closed the door. She ran to the window and looked out, watching her daddy get into the car. She watched as he drove away in their blue sedan. Kristen walked into the kitchen where her mom was washing breakfast dishes and pulled on her mother's skirt to get her mom's attention.

"Mommy, Daddy said goodbye," said Kristen.

Caroline looked down at Kristen and smiled. She dried her hands and then hugged Kristen saying, "You're the best thing that has ever happened to your father and me. Princess, we love you so much. How about after I finish the dishes, I read you a story? We'll make Daddy something special for supper tonight before going to the zoo. Is that a good idea?"

"Yes, that is a good idea," answered Kristen.

Forty-five minutes passed. Kristen and her mom were sitting on the couch when the doorbell rang. Caroline got off the couch and looked out the door window. She quickly opened the door when she saw two policemen standing on the doorstep. One officer was tall and thinly built. The other officer was tall and husky.

"May we speak to Mrs. Winters?" asked the tall, thin Officer Telly.

Caroline stood there numb and said, "I'm Mrs. Winters. What has happened?"

"My name is Officer Telly, and this is my partner, Officer Mitchell. Mrs. Winters, you should sit down. What we are going to tell you isn't going to be good. It's about your husband. There was an accident," explained Officer Telly. Caroline looked at Officer Telly, went to the couch, and sat down next to Kristen. Officer Telly followed her and said, "Your husband had internal injuries, and I'm sorry, but he didn't make it. He died instantly. I'm sorry we're not here with better news, Mrs. Winters. We need you to come down to the morgue to identify him. The driver that hit your husband's car had been pulled over before for drinking and driving. This is his second offense, so he will be charged with homicide by intoxication while operating a motor vehicle. He will be facing a possible maximum of forty years in prison. He is on his way to jail as we speak. I'm really sorry that we had to come here. I wish it were under better circumstances."

Caroline started sobbing; tears rolled down her cheeks. Kristen looked at her mom crying and started to get scared.

"What's wrong, Mommy? Are we in trouble, Mommy?" asked Kristen.

"No, Princess, we have to go to the hospital. The policemen are going to take us," answered Caroline.

"Why, Mommy, are you sick?" asked Kristen.

"No, Princess, Mommy will tell you later," answered Caroline. Caroline walked to the closet and grabbed her jacket and Kristen's soft pink cotton jacket.

"Here, let me help you get your daughter's jacket on. What is her name?" asked Officer Telly as he took the jacket from Caroline.

"Thank you, her name is Kristen," answered Caroline.

Officer Telly put the jacket on Kristen and started talking to her. "You and your mommy are going to get a ride to the hospital in the police car. There is nothing to be scared of Kristen," said Officer Telly. He grabbed Kristen's hand and walked to the door. Caroline and officer Mitchell followed slowly behind them. On their way to the hospital, Kristen sat in front of Officer Telly. Caroline was in the back seat crying. She tried not to cry too loudly so Kristen wouldn't hear her. Officer Mitchell tried to calm Caroline down before they got to the hospital.

By the time they arrived, Caroline had calmed down. Kristen was laughing at a joke Officer Telly had told her, unaware of what her mom was talking about in the back seat. They entered the hospital, and Officer Telly spoke to Caroline and his partner, "Officer Mitchell will take you where you have to go, Mrs. Winters. I'll stay here with Kristen so she doesn't see this, okay?"

"That's a good idea, Telly. We shouldn't be too long," said Officer Mitchell.

Caroline and Officer Mitchell walked down the hall to the elevator to go to the morgue. Kristen watched as her mom walked away with the other policeman.

"Mr. Telly, where is my mommy going?" asked Kristen.

"Your mom is going to see your dad. She'll be back in a while, Kristen," answered Officer Telly.

"Can we go see my daddy? Why didn't Mommy take me to see Daddy too?" asked Kristen.

"Your daddy is in bad shape. You have to be strong, Kristen, for your mommy. Your mommy needs you to help her get through this. Can you be strong for your mommy, Kristen?" asked Officer Telly.

"Yes, Daddy says I'm strong like Mommy," said Kristen.

"Kristen, how about you and I go to the cafeteria and get a scoop of ice cream? What kind of ice cream do you like, Kristen?" asked Officer Telly.

"I like strawberry ice cream, Mr. Telly. Can I get two scoops on it?" asked Kristen.

"Sure, let's go and get us some ice cream," answered Officer Telly.

They walked to the elevator and pressed the button. When they got down to the cafeteria, they sat at a table close to the entrance. Officer Telly asked the waitress for two strawberry ice cream cones. He handed the waitress some money. Three minutes later, she came back with two double scooped strawberry ice cream cones. She handed Kristen one and gave Officer Telly his. Kristen started to talk to Officer Telly.

"What happens if Mommy comes back, and we're not there?" asked Kristen.

"Well, I'll just grab this radio here and talk to my partner to let him know where we are, okay?" asked Officer Telly. He had a grin on his face as he called his partner. He told Officer Mitchell where he and Kristen were. Officer Telly asked Officer Mitchell how much longer it would take. Officer Mitchell told him at least fifteen minutes. Officer Telly looked at Kristen who was watching him. He tried to keep a smile on his face so Kristen wouldn't know something was wrong. Officer Telly could tell by the tone of his partner's voice that things weren't good. He knew Kristen's mom was really upset and in shock from what she had seen. He knew it would take his partner at least fifteen minutes to calm her down. He started eating his ice cream cone. Kristen watched him quietly as she ate hers. After they were done, they sat there laughing. Officer Telly was telling her kid jokes to get her to laugh, and it worked. Time went by fast as they both waited for Officer Mitchell and Kristen's mom.

Soon Caroline and Officer Mitchell were in the cafeteria sitting at the table with Kristen across on the other side of the table. Caroline's eyes were extremely red from crying.

"Mommy, Mr. Telly and I had a strawberry ice cream cone. Mommy, can I go see Daddy too?" asked Kristen.

"Princess, Daddy didn't make it, honey. Daddy is in heaven now, sweetie. Daddy won't be coming home with us, Princess," explained Caroline with tears in her eyes.

"Mommy, what do you mean? Daddy is staying here? Why?" asked Kristen.

Officer Telly was still sitting next to Kristen, and he looked at Caroline as tears rolled down her cheeks. He decided to jump into the conversation to help Caroline out.

"Kristen, your daddy didn't get better. He got worse. Your daddy was hurt really bad in a car accident. The doctors couldn't help your daddy. Your daddy was hurt too badly, so your daddy was taken to heaven. He'll always be watching over you, but you won't see him anymore because he's an angel now. Your mommy needs you to help her by understanding. Do you understand what I'm saying Kristen?" asked Officer Telly.

"Daddy won't ever come home? I want Daddy to come home tonight," said Kristen.

"Princess, Daddy can't come home. Daddy is dead," explained Caroline.

Kristen started crying. Caroline picked Kristen up and hugged her. Caroline looked at the two officers. Both officers were getting teary-eyed. They were touched by Kristen's actions.

Kristen looked at Officer Telly and said, "Mr. Telly, can you bring my daddy back, please?" begged Kristen.

Officer Telly looked at Kristen and saw a desperate little child. "Kristen, if I could bring your dad back, I would, but I can't. I don't have the means of doing such a thing. You feel a lot of pain right now, but eventually it will get easier. It will take time. Your mom needs you now more than ever," explained Officer Telly.

Caroline stood watching. She heard them from a distance. It felt like she was far away from her body, and she felt so numb.

"We have to go home now, Kristen. We've kept Officer Telly and Officer Mitchell from their job long enough. Thank you for giving us a ride and spending some time with Kristen so I could go to the morgue," said Caroline.

"We'll take you and Kristen home, okay, Mrs. Winters?" said Officer Mitchell.

"Yes, that would be very nice. Thank you," said Caroline.

Officer Telly grabbed Kristen's hand and started walking out of the cafeteria. Caroline and Officer Mitchell walked slowly behind them talking.

On their way home, Kristen sat up front with Officer Telly while Caroline sat in the back, talking to Officer Mitchell. Officer Telly and Officer Mitchell dropped them off.

Once home, Kristen hugged her mommy and said, "Mommy, Daddy has some presents in the closet for us. He was going to give them to us tonight."

Caroline looked at Kristen and almost started bawling. She hugged Kristen as they walked to the closet. They looked up at the shelf above the coat rack where there were two presents, one for Kristen and one for Caroline. Caroline grabbed the presents. She smiled, then grabbed Kristen's hand as they sat on the couch. Kristen opened hers first. There were two Barbie dolls. Caroline opened hers, and it was a gold bracelet with an inscription that read, "To my gorgeous queen, may our love last forever." Caroline looked at Kristen with a smile on her face, attempting to hide how she really felt.

"Princess, let's have something to eat. How does peanut butter and jelly sound?" asked Caroline.

"That sounds good. Mommy, are we still going to the zoo tonight even though Daddy isn't coming home?" asked Kristen.

"No, Princess, Mommy is really tired. We'll go tomorrow, okay?" said Caroline.

Weeks went by, and Caroline became depressed. The first year was the roughest. Kristen began having nightmares and would wake up screaming and crying for her dad. Caroline awakened almost every night to Kristen's screams.

"Daddy, come back. Don't leave me and Mommy," screamed Kristen.

When Caroline went to Kristen's room, Kristen was crying, and sweat rolled down her face. "Mommy, why won't Daddy come home? I want Daddy to come home," said Kristen.

"Princess, Daddy is in heaven now. In spirit, he'll always be with us," said Caroline.

Kristen was too young to understand that her dad wasn't coming home. Every day she sat by the window watching and waiting for him. Caroline watched Kristen as she sat by the window daily. It broke her heart to see her daughter waiting for him. She was concerned about Kristen, her frequent nightmares. Caroline tried explaining to Kristen that her dad wasn't coming home, but Kristen wouldn't accept it.

This went on for months until Caroline took Kristen to a psychologist. He told Caroline only time would make Kristen realize her dad wasn't coming back. Kristen continued seeing the psychologist once a month.

As the years went by, Kristen finally accepted that her dad wasn't coming home. She turned into a very angry child, becoming moody and having outbursts in class. The teachers would have to take Kristen out in the hall to calm her down. Caroline attended the parent-teacher conference every other week.

Every Father's Day the teachers would have the children make their dads Father's Day cards. Kristen would destroy the other children's cards. She felt angry because they had dads, and she didn't. Caroline was frustrated and highly depressed, so she began drinking more excessively. When her husband was alive, they were lucky if they drank once every six months. Now Caroline was drinking all weekend. She thought drinking would help her deal with what was going on with everyday life. She hated coming home to an empty house, and she missed her husband so much she felt like she had died three years ago with him.

When Kristen turned thirteen, she started pushing kids around. She would have violent rages, and the teachers would call Caroline at work to come and take Kristen home. Kristen was getting into more trouble.

Two years went by, and when Kristen turned fifteen years old, she was alone on her birthday. Caroline was always in a bar after work. She left Kristen the phone number of the bar on the refrigerator in case Kristen needed to get hold of her. Caroline didn't spend much time with her daughter because Kristen reminded her of Jeff. Whenever Caroline thought of Jeff, she got depressed.

It was cold that night in the middle of December when Kristen was walking down the street with her best friend Cheyenne. "What did you think of that party, Cheyenne?" asked Kristen.

"It was great! Except there was too much drinking, Kristen. I think you drank too much too. What if your mom finds out you've been drinking?"

"My mom won't care at all. She's with her friends at the bar! She doesn't even know I'm alive. All she cares about is her bar friends," said Kristen.

Kristen and Cheyenne were almost to Cheyenne's house when their friend Sasha, who went to school with them, ran into them. Sasha talked them into going to another party. The three girls walked a couple of blocks down the street. Sasha said, "We're almost there, you guys. It's four more houses down."

They went up some stairs and knocked on the door. A young man named Chris, who looked like he was in his midthirties, opened the door.

"We're here for the party!" Sasha said.

He let the girls in. "Do you want a beer, Sasha?" Chris asked.

"Yeah, sure, why not! One can't do too much damage I guess," said Sasha.

"Do your two friends want a beer too?" he asked.

"They sure do!" answered Sasha.

Cheyenne looked at Sasha and shook her head and said, "Sasha, I don't like to drink, and I don't think Kristen should have any more to drink either!"

"Kristen couldn't get any drunker than she is now, right, Cheyenne?" asked Sasha.

"Yes, I guess you're right," Cheyenne said back.

Chris, who was standing right next to them, handed Kristen and Sasha a beer. After an hour passed, Cheyenne began to look worried about Kristen, who was barely standing.

Meanwhile, Sasha was in the back room getting high on marijuana. Cheyenne went up to Sasha and said, "Sasha, we have to get Kristen out of here. She's really in bad shape." Sasha nodded in agreement with Cheyenne. They walked up to Kristen. Cheyenne was on one side of Kristen, and Sasha was on the other side holding her up. Sasha figured they better get Kristen home, so they took a shortcut around the lake. They walked on the sidewalk until they saw a dock. Kristen, Cheyenne, and Sasha walked to the end of the dock and sat down. They sat for a few minutes and Cheyenne said, "Sasha, I want to talk to you for a minute alone, okay?" The two girls stood up and walked to the front of the dock and talked while Kristen sat at the end of the dock. They were trying to figure out a way to get Kristen home since she couldn't even walk on her own. They continued conversing until they heard a splash. It sounded like it came from the direction where Kristen was sitting. Cheyenne and Sasha looked at the end of the dock. Neither of the two girls could see her! *Where was Kristen?* they were both thinking to themselves.

They ran to the end of the dock and saw Kristen struggling to stay above the icy waters. Cheyenne and Sasha knew Kristen didn't know how to swim.

Kristen went deeper into the freezing cold water under the ice. The water felt as cold as a thousand ice cubes with sharp edges on them put together, all in one spot of her skin. Multiply it by a trillion times all over her body! All of her skin felt like it was getting cut at the same time.

She struggled to get up to the top surface of the lake. The lake was so cold, and Kristen was becoming weaker and weaker by the minute. Her body was getting numb. Water was forcing its way down her throat and into her lungs. Kristen could hardly feel herself move; her body was so numb. She was losing touch with reality. She kept ending up on the top surface of the lake; then she would end up down on the bottom of the lake. She kept struggling on and off as her vision turned black. The water was smothering her. Kristen was to the point where she was as weak as she could get. She was exhausted and barely moving. She didn't know what was reality anymore. Kristen didn't know what was happening. *Who was she? Where was she?* Those thoughts ran through her mind. She couldn't breathe much longer. Suddenly it turned black. It was like she was dead. She couldn't think nor see nor could she feel anything. It was pitch black. The icy water finally succeeded in getting the best of her. She was gone for a while in a place where nobody could help her. It was a place of darkness. It was like nothing existed in the world. Kristen was lifeless.

Cheyenne dove into the icy cold water to find Kristen. Pulling Kristen up with her, she grabbed the limp body and swam up to the surface. Cheyenne lifted her lifeless friend up to Sasha who was standing on the end of the dock. Sasha grabbed Kristen's seemingly lifeless arms and lifted her up onto the dock. Sasha set the pale-faced body carefully onto the dock. Then she helped Cheyenne get out of the water onto the dock. "We have to get Kristen to a hospital. She is barely breathing, Sasha!" said Cheyenne.

"Stay here! I'll go for help!" said Sasha. Sasha ran to the closest house half a block from the lake. It was a red brick house with black shutters on it. Sasha knocked on the door, trembling from the cold weather. The door opened, and a young man with brown hair appeared inside the doorway. Sasha explained what had happened. The young man told Sasha to call the police on the phone in the living room and told her to wait there. He ran upstairs and grabbed four blankets. Hurrying down the stairs, the young man handed Sasha two blankets and said, "We have to get these blankets to your friends immediately. Take me to where your friends are, please. We have to hurry!"

Back on the dock, Cheyenne sat next to her best friend. Kristen wasn't moving at all. The color in her skin was gone, and she looked so lifeless. She was as pale as a ghost. Cheyenne realized if Kristen didn't get immediate medical assistance, Cheyenne would lose her best friend. Cheyenne's clothes were so damp and cold. Her body was getting so numb, and she started getting tired. She was getting sleepier and sleepier every minute; she started to lose touch with reality until she heard a noise that brought her back to reality. Cheyenne turned and looked at Kristen lying so still on the dock and then turned to look toward the street. She saw Sasha and a young man with blankets running toward Kristen and her. Cheyenne felt herself drifting off to sleep. Then her vision went black; the darkness overtook her.

Officer Telly and Officer Mitchell showed up at the scene. They had two wool blankets in the trunk of their squad. Officer Telly grabbed one and ran to the end of the dock. Officer Mitchell followed with the other blanket and laid the wool blanket over the other blankets on Cheyenne. Officer Telly laid the wool blanket he had over the other blankets that covered Kristen. He stared at Kristen for the longest time, she looked familiar. Then he remembered who she was. It was ten years ago when her father had been killed by a drunken driver. He started to talk to Officer Mitchell. "Mitchell, this is Kristen Winters. We answered a call ten years ago when her father had been killed by a drunken driver. Do you remember the little girl that begged me to bring her dad back, but I couldn't? I told her I didn't have the means to do so."

"Yes, I remember now! Your right, Telly. Oh my god, no," said Officer Mitchell.

Officer Telly looked at Kristen barely breathing and leaned down by her side and started talking to her, "Kristen, you can't give up. Do you hear me, Kristen? Don't give up. You have too much to live for. I'll make a deal with you. If you don't give up, I'll take you to the ice cream shop down by the cafeteria at the hospital. I'll take you to get a double scoop strawberry ice cream cone when you get better. Please, Kristen, you got to keep fighting for your life." Finally, minutes later, the paramedics arrived.

Cheyenne woke up four hours later in the hospital. Sasha was sitting in a chair next to the hospital bed where her friend Cheyenne was lying. "Sasha, where is Kristen? What happened? Why am I in the hospital?" asked Cheyenne.

"Oh, thank God you're okay, Cheyenne! Kristen is in a coma, and she also lost a lot of blood. She must have hit her head against the dock before she fell into the lake. The freezing water and ice didn't help matters at all. Cheyenne, you are in the hospital because you passed out when we got to the dock. The doctor examined you while you were unconscious to make sure you were all right. He said you could leave after you awaken," explained Sasha.

Cheyenne got out of the hospital bed, got dressed, and Sasha and Cheyenne headed toward the door. As they walked down the hall, Cheyenne said, "Sasha, what floor and room is Kristen on?"

"Kristen is on the third floor in room 303. She's in critical condition. I want to warn you, she isn't going to look that great. She doesn't look like the Kristen we know," said Sasha.

Cheyenne and Sasha waited for the elevator, and they got into the elevator and pushed the third-floor button. The elevator started moving, and they were on their way up to see Kristen. When they entered Kristen's room, they saw her lifeless body lying there in the hospital bed. The color in Kristen's skin was gone, and she was as pale as a ghost. She had a bandage that went all the way around her forehead. There was a heart monitor on the table next to her bed. The doctors had four round flat plastic heartbeat sensors that were hooked up to the heart monitor. Kristen had the heartbeat sensor taped on her chest. Tubes were connected to needles that went into her arms. She also had a big tube that went to her mouth. Cheyenne and Sasha sat in the two chairs next to Kristen. Kristen looked very weak and her eyes had black and blue circles around them. Cheyenne and Sasha got up, stood in the doorway, and started whispering.

"Sasha, did the police call her mom? Is she on her way here?" asked Cheyenne.

"No, the police couldn't find her, Cheyenne! I told them where they might find her, so they went to Phil's Bar. The bartender said she had left one hour ago, and he didn't know where she went. The police told the bartender that if she came back, to let her know that her daughter was in the hospital."

"I sure hope her mom shows up here soon. Kristen needs her mom more than ever now," said Sasha. Cheyenne and Sasha stared at Kristen for a long time. They didn't know what to say to Kristen, and if they did say something to Kristen, they wondered if she would even hear them.

As Kristen lay in the hospital bed unconscious, thoughts ran through her mind. She remembered when she was five years old, the last day she saw her dad.

He told her they were going to the zoo after he got home from work. He said, "Kristen, I have to fix some of the computers at work for my boss. I have a present for you and your mother. I picked up the presents yesterday after work. Don't tell Mommy, okay? I want it to be a surprise. Well, I'm going to be late for work if I don't leave now. How about a hug for daddy, Half-pint?" She watched him as he picked up his briefcase. Then he turned the doorknob, opened the door, turned around, looked at Kristen, and waved goodbye. Kristen waved goodbye back at him as he closed the door. Kristen ran to the window and looked out, watching her dad get in the car and drive away in the blue sedan. Her mom was in the kitchen washing the breakfast dishes. Kristen walked into the kitchen near the sink, stood next to her mother, and pulled on the bottom of her mom's skirt to get her attention.

"Mommy, Daddy says goodbye."

Her mom looked down at her and smiled. She dried her hands and hugged Kristen and said, "You're the best thing that has ever happened to your father and me. We love you so much. How about after I finish the dishes, I'll read you a story? We'll make Daddy something special for supper tonight before we go to the zoo. Is that a good idea?"

"Yes, that's a good idea," answered Kristen. Kristen's memory started to fade.

Cheyenne and Sasha were looking at their friend. "Cheyenne, it is getting late. We should go home," said Sasha.

"Yeah, I guess you're right. I should call my parents. Sasha, you should too," said Cheyenne.

"Yes, I know. I'm going to call my mom and dad now. Want to come with me, Cheyenne?" asked Sasha.

As Cheyenne and Sasha left the room, Cheyenne said, "Bye, Kristen. I'll come back as soon as I can."

Sasha closed the door to Kristen's room, and Cheyenne followed. As Cheyenne and Sasha were leaving, a nurse went in to check on Kristen. Cheyenne started crying when she left the room where her best friend was lying motionless. Sasha and Cheyenne were walking to the elevator when they heard someone call out their names. Sasha and Cheyenne stopped and turned around to see who called their names. It was a nurse. The nurse walked toward them and told them their parents were waiting for them down in the lobby on the first floor. They turned back around and headed for the elevator. The elevator door was open, so Cheyenne and Sasha walked into the elevator and pushed the first-floor button. "Sasha, if the police don't find Kristen's mom, Kristen might give up and quit fighting for her life. We have to find her. We owe Kristen at least that much, wouldn't you say?" Cheyenne said.

Sasha looked at Cheyenne, then said, "Yes, I agree with you. Kristen needs all of us to be here for her, especially her mom."

The elevator door opened on the first floor. Cheyenne and Sasha saw their parents sitting in the chairs next to the door with the brightly lit red "Exit" sign. The girls sat down next to their parents and explained what had happened. Their parents told them they had already heard the whole story. Cheyenne hugged her parents and left so they could get some rest. Sasha and her parents left shortly thereafter.

As everybody was leaving the hospital, Kristen started having another flashback. She was lying motionless in the hospital bed and was very weak. Off and on the darkness would take over. She would have different visions of when she was growing up. She started having a flashback of when she was sitting on the dock. It was so cold it overtook her. She lost her balance, and it caused her to fall. As she fell, she hit her head against the edge of the dock, hitting the icy water. The flashback started to fade to a different flashback where she was with her mom sitting on the couch, and her mom was reading her a story. Then Kristen remembered when she saw her dad walk out the door with his briefcase. She remembered the last words her father said, "See ya later, Half-pint," and how forty-five minutes later, Kristen and her mom were sitting on the couch when the doorbell rang. Kristen's mom got up and walked to the door, and she looked out through the door window. She quickly opened the door when she saw two policemen standing on the doorsteps.

"May we speak to Mrs. Winters?" asked the police officer.

"I'm Mrs. Winters. What has happened?" asked her mom.

"Mrs. Winters, you should sit down. What we are going to tell you isn't going to be good. It's about your husband. There was an accident," said the officer.

Her mom goes to the couch where Kristen was sitting and sat down beside her. The police officer was telling her mom that her dad was killed. Kristen was too young to understand what was happening. The police officer started talking, "Your husband had internal injuries, and I'm sorry, but he didn't make it. He died instantly. Your husband was killed twenty minutes ago in an accident. The driver that hit your husband's car had been pulled over before for drinking and driving. This is his second offense, so he will be charged with homicide by the intoxication of a motor vehicle. He is on his way to jail as we speak," explained the police officer. That's how Kristen remembered it. Kristen's memory started to fade.

The police found Kristen's mom, and she was sitting next to Kristen's bed. Caroline had been there for two days now. She had tears in her eyes as she looked at her daughter lying motionless in the hospital bed. Kristen's condition had gotten worse. Her lungs had collapsed, so the doctor had to hook her up to a respirator to help her breathe.

Caroline felt so helpless. She hadn't felt this way since she had lost Kristen's dad, Jeff. "Kristen, I'm here, my little princess. You'll be okay. I know after your dad died, I didn't treat you very well. I neglected you by not paying enough attention to you. I should have spent more time with you because if I did, you wouldn't be here right now. I should have spent more time with you instead of drinking alcohol at the bars. You're my little princess, and I'm so sorry for the way it's been for you. Please forgive me. Your father left us when he had just turned thirty-four. Please don't leave me as your father did. I don't know what I would do without you. It's bad enough I lost your father. I don't want to lose you too. You're still my little princess. I promise you it will be different when you wake up. If you can hear me, I want to make a promise to you. I promise I'll quit drinking. I can remember when your dad was alive. We were a really close family, and when your dad died, we drifted apart because of my drinking. Kristen, please don't die on me!" begged Caroline.

Three days went by. Cheyenne's parents brought her and Sasha to the hospital to visit Kristen. There was no change in Kristen's condition. Officer Telly and Officer Mitchell stopped regularly every day after work. They would visit her and try to encourage her to keep fighting. They were hoping her condition would get better.

Caroline sat by Kristen's side and didn't leave her unless someone was in visiting Kristen. When Caroline got tired, she slept in the chair. Six days later, in the morning, when Caroline awakened at 5:00 a.m., she looked at Kristen, and then she held her hand. A nurse came in and looked at the heart monitor. Kristen's heart was extremely slow and was getting slower.

The nurse ran out of the room to find a doctor. Minutes later, the nurse and two doctors came back. They brought in a defibrillator.

While the nurse was in the hall getting the doctors, Kristen's heart had stopped beating. Caroline was aware of what was happening. Kristen was dying. Caroline started crying; she felt numb, and the doctors hooked the machine up and tried to get Kristen's heart started. All Caroline could hear was the doctors saying, "Clear." Caroline was in a daze.

During this time, Kristen had a vision she was walking through a tunnel. At the end of the tunnel, there was beautiful, bright, sky-blue light. When she got to the end of the tunnel, her dad was standing in the light. Jeff didn't even look like he had aged from the last day Kristen had seen him. He looked like he did the day he had died. Kristen ran up to her dad and gave him a hug. Kristen's dad started to talk. "Kristen, you have to go back. Half-pint, it's not your time yet! Your mom needs you. I love you, Half-pint, and I'll miss you. But it isn't your time yet." Tears ran down Kristen's cheeks.

"Daddy, I love you," said Kristen.

"I love you too, and I always will. I'm with you and your mom all the time. Wherever you go, I'll always be with you in your heart. Oh, by the way, Half-pint, a man in a uniform was with you and your mom the day I died. He was also there with your mom and me the day you were born. He'll be coming back in your lives to help. You and your mom will get past this, and he will help you and your mom move on. He'll take care of both of you, and he'll love you unconditionally, if you give him a chance. Tell your mom it's okay to move on and love again. I want her to start living again. I want your mom to be loved and happy. I'll always be watching over you and your mom and the man in the uniform. You must hurry. Go, Half-pint!" said her dad.

Kristen hugged her dad one last time, turned around, and walked back into the tunnel away from her dad in the beautiful, bright, sky-blue light.

The doctors were getting frustrated because they were trying so hard to get Kristen's heart started. Caroline stood in the back of the room crying, watching as the doctors worked on Kristen. Suddenly, her heart started beating. It was a success. Kristen's heart started beating by itself again.

Three days later, at ten in the morning, Kristen came out of the coma. Slowly her condition improved. Officer Telly was sitting next to Kristen's hospital bed when Kristen came out of the coma. Caroline was exhausted, so when Officer Telly came to Kristen's room, he told Caroline to go home and get some rest. He was sitting there in the chair remembering when he was a rookie cop and he had gotten a call. It was before Kristen was born when he went to her house for the first time. When he got there, Caroline was on the kitchen floor in premature labor. Blood was all over the kitchen floor where Caroline lay unconscious. Jeff was holding her head in his lap. He had such fear in his eyes, and his eyes were bloodshot from crying. When Jeff saw Officer Telly, he looked at him and said, "Please help my wife and my baby. Don't let them die. They are all I have. Please don't let them die."

At that moment, Officer Telly felt helpless because there was nothing he could do; he wasn't a doctor. All they could do was wait for the ambulance. Suddenly he heard someone talking to him, bringing him back to reality.

"Mr. Telly, can I have a double-scooped strawberry ice cream cone? Where is my mom?" asked Kristen. Officer Telly looked down at Kristen with a huge grin on his face. He was so happy that Kristen was awake that his eyes started watering. He pushed the nurse's button so she could check Kristen.

"Kristen, thank God you're all right! You gave us quite a scare. Officer Mitchell and I were worried about you. Your mom was exhausted, so I told her to go home and get some sleep and that I would stay here with you until she came back. Tomorrow is my day off, so I figured I would stay here. Officer Mitchell is going to stop tomorrow to visit you. Your mom has been with you since shortly after you were brought here," explained Officer Telly.

"Where am I? How long have I been here? You promised you would take me to have a double-scooped ice cream cone. Did you mean it?" asked Kristen.

"Yes, I did mean it. How did you know? You have been in a coma for quite a while. Kristen, could you hear me?" asked Officer Telly.

"Mr. Telly, I could hear Officer Mitchell, and my mom and you talking off and on. I could understand very little. I understood what you were saying when you promised me some ice cream when I got better. I feel extremely hungry and tired," said Kristen.

"Kristen, you should rest so when your mom gets here, you can surprise her. I'll talk to you more after you wake up, okay?" said Officer Telly.

Kristen agreed and then closed her eyes and fell asleep. When the nurse came in to check on Kristen, Officer Telly left the room and called his partner to tell Mitchell Kristen had come out of the coma. He told Mitchell not to call Caroline because she needed some sleep. Besides, he wanted her to be surprised when she came back to the hospital and found her daughter awake.

Caroline showed up at the hospital at 3:00 p.m., and when she walked up to the door to Kristen's room, she looked into the glass window on the right side of the door. She saw Officer Telly sitting next to Kristen's bed. He had fallen asleep. She walked into the room as quietly as possible so she wouldn't wake Officer Telly. Caroline stood at the end of the bed. She looked at Kristen who seemed to have more color to her face. When Kristen sensed someone was staring at her, she opened her eyes. At first, Caroline flinched and backed up into the wall because it freaked her out. When she backed into the wall, it was loud enough to wake Officer Telly. She wasn't expecting her daughter's eyes to open. Caroline looked at Kristen. Then she turned to see if she had awakened Officer Telly. He was staring at her with a grin on his face. Caroline's face turned beet red from embarrassment.

"Caroline, is something wrong?" asked Officer Telly as he smiled at her.

"I'm sorry, I didn't mean to wake you up. It's just that Kristen's eyes opened, and it kind of freaked me out," explained Caroline.

"That's okay. I was just resting my eyes. I wasn't really in a deep sleep. You look like you are well rested, if I do say so myself. I see getting some sleep agrees with you, Caroline. You look great," said Officer Telly.

"Thank you, Officer Telly. You're too kind. How is Kristen? Has there been any change?" asked Caroline.

"You can call me Steve, Caroline. I'm the wrong person to be asking if she is okay. You should be asking Kristen herself. She came out of the coma this morning shortly after you left. I didn't call you because I wanted you to get some sleep. I hope you're not mad at me," said Officer Telly.

"That's okay, Steve, I'm not mad at you at all. I needed to rest so I could be here for Kristen. Thank you so much for everything you have done for me and Kristen," said Caroline.

Kristen was staring at her mom and Officer Telly with a grin on her face. Caroline looked at Kristen's smiling face. Officer Telly moved his chair closer to Kristen's bed and saw Kristen's amusement with him and her mom. He started to chuckle.

"Mom, I'm sorry I worried you. I didn't mean to put you through this," Kristen said.

"Kristen, I love you so much it doesn't matter. The only thing that matters is that you are all right now. I have had a lot of time to think about why this had happened, about how my drinking had gotten out of hand, and how I wasn't paying enough attention to you. I'm so sorry for what I put you through. Steve has been here almost every day waiting for you to get better."

"I know, Mom. Mr. Telly and I were talking this morning, and he is really nice," said Kristen.

Listening with a grin on his face, Steve looked at Kristen and Caroline. He thought to himself how Kristen looked so much like Caroline, as long jet-black hair relaxed on their shoulders and how beautiful their blue eyes were. Kristen looked like Caroline did when he first saw her fifteen years ago, only younger.

Through the weeks to come, Steve started to grow attached to Caroline and Kristen. Kristen was getting better. They took the respirator and the heart monitor off. Kristen started going to therapy. On Officer Telly's next day off, he went to the hospital early. Officer Telly talked to the nurse earlier and asked if Kristen was well enough to take her down to the ice cream shop. The nurse told Officer Telly Kristen had therapy at noon, but after she got back from therapy, he could take her down to the ice cream shop. Caroline spent the night before at the hospital, and she slept in the chair next to Kristen's bed. When the nurse took Kristen to therapy, Caroline went home to take a shower and change.

After therapy, the nurse pushed Kristen's wheelchair to her room. When Officer Telly walked into Kristen's room, she was waiting in the wheelchair, staring at the wall. She looked really bored.

"Kristen, do you feel up to going down to the ice cream shop?" asked Officer Telly.

"Yes, that would be nice. I have been looking forward to having a double-scooped strawberry ice cream cone," answered Kristen.

When they got to the ice cream shop, they went to a table. Officer Telly ordered the ice cream cones, then said to Kristen, "Your mother has been doing really well at not drinking."

"Mr. Telly, is it okay if I call you Steve?" asked Kristen

"Of course you can, Kristen, I was wondering why you weren't calling me Steve a few days ago," answered Officer Telly.

"Steve, can you help my mom? She needs someone besides me to help her get through this. She needs to know someone else cares besides me. I'm so proud of my mom. She is trying so hard. She goes to an Alcoholics Anonymous meeting tonight. I'm worried that things are going to get a lot rougher for her because when she is sober, she starts thinking of my dad. She'll get depressed, and it could make her have a relapse. She could start drinking again," said Kristen.

"Kristen, I had planned on asking your mom if I could go with her to some of the meetings. I don't plan on walking out of your lives. The only way I'll walk out of your lives is if you and your mom ask me to," said Officer Telly.

"Good, because we have grown fond of you and Officer Mitchell. My mom seems happier when you are around," said Kristen.

"Kristen, I'll be here for you and Caroline as long as you need me. If your mom lets me, I'll go with her to the meeting tonight. Your mom has a lot of healing to do. All we can do is be there for her. It'll work out for your mom. She just needs a shoulder to lean on. I'll be that shoulder if she lets me. I've grown very fond of you and Caroline. Is it a deal, Kristen?" asked Officer Telly.

"That sounds good to me, Steve, but will you promise me?" asked Kristen.

"Yes, Kristen, I can and I will promise you that I'll be there for you and your mom," answered Officer Telly. As Officer Telly said that, his eyes twinkled. They ate their ice cream cones and headed back to Kristen's room. When they arrived, Caroline was reading a book.

Kristen looked at Officer Telly and saw how his eyes lit up when he saw Caroline. She knew Steve was really starting to care about her mom. Kristen started smiling. When Caroline realized they were back from eating ice cream, she put a bookmarker in her book and put it on the table next to Kristen's bed. Caroline looked at Officer Telly and at Kristen. They both were smiling.

"How was your ice cream, Steve and Kristen?" asked Caroline.

"It was really good. You should have come with us, Caroline," said Officer Telly.

"Good, I would've been here sooner, but I was looking for something at home. It took me a while to find what I was looking for, but I finally found it. Kristen, it is something you used to have with you at all times until you started getting older," said Caroline. She opened the brown paper bag and pulled out the teddy bear that was given to Kristen when she was a baby on the day Jeff and Caroline brought her home from the hospital. When Caroline handed it to Kristen, her eyes lit up. When Kristen was growing up, it was her favorite teddy bear.

"Mom, I didn't know we still had this teddy bear. This is the one the doctors and nurses gave me when you and Daddy brought me home from the hospital, isn't it?" asked Kristen.

"Yes, it is, Princess. After you got older, I washed it and put it away for safekeeping. I figured someday you would need it again. I know you are getting older, but it missed you. Seeing as how I can't be with you all the time, I figured you would need an old friend to keep you safe," said Caroline.

Officer Telly was daydreaming of Caroline and him when he realized Caroline and Kristen were both staring at him funny.

Quickly he says, "I'm sorry, ladies. Were you talking to me? I seemed to have gotten sidetracked."

Caroline burst out laughing because they knew he was daydreaming of something. Because when he was daydreaming, he was chuckling out loud. He had such a big grin on his face.

"So, Caroline, would it offend you if I asked you if I could go to the meeting tonight with you?" asked Officer Telly.

"I think it would be a great idea, Steve, but who's going to be here with Kristen?" asked Caroline.

"Officer Mitchell is going to be here after work, so Kristen won't be alone. You don't mind Kristen, do you?" asked Officer Telly.

"No, I don't mind at all. I like Officer Mitchell. He's really nice," answered Kristen. "Mom, thanks for bringing Teddy here. As long as I have Teddy, I'll be fine. Yes, I'm sure, Mom."

"Okay then, Steve, I'll be looking forward to having you come with me to the meeting tonight," said Caroline smiling.

When Mike got to the hospital, he started talking to Steve Telly, "Steve, how is Kristen? Is she all right with me staying with her while you and Caroline are at the Alcoholics Anonymous meeting?"

"Yes, Kristen thinks it'll be fun. She thinks you're really nice," said Steve.

"My wife, Janette, wants to meet Caroline and Kristen. Next time I come to visit Kristen, Janette wants to come with me. Do you think it'll be all right?" asked Mike.

"I think it would be great for Kristen and Caroline. A person can never have too many friends," said Steve.

Steve moved closer to Caroline with a grin. "Caroline, it's about that time. We should get going soon," said Steve.

Caroline looked at him and said, "Yes, you're right, Steve. We should get going." She walked over to Kristen and gave her a big hug and said, "Well, I got to go now, Princess. I don't want to be late. I love you so much. I'll see you when I get back."

"I understand, Mom. I really do. Hey, Mom, I'm really proud of you, and I love you too," said Kristen.

As Caroline and Steve walked out of the room, they both smiled at Kristen. Steve decided to take Caroline to the ice cream shop for an ice cream cone. Steve and Caroline sat and talked and laughed and had fun. After a while, they realized it was getting late so they headed back to Kristen's room. Caroline and Steve were in the hall near Kristen's room when they noticed Mike and Kristen were playing cards. Caroline and Steve stopped walking and watched Mike and Kristen. Kristen and Mike started laughing.

"Looks like we weren't the only ones who had fun," said Steve.

"Yes, you're right. It looks like my little princess has been having fun too. She's really good at card games. She can always beat the pants off of me," said Caroline.

"I know what you mean. That's what happens to me too when I play cards with her. Caroline, can I ask you a question?" said Steve.

"Sure you can," said Caroline.

"Caroline, how did Kristen learn how to play cards the way she does?"

"Her dad taught her. Jeff and Kristen played cards every day before supper. By age five, she knew how to play poker, King's Corner, Spades, and War. Kristen is a quick learner. She's very smart. But after Jeff died, she started having nightmares. She refused to learn more than she wanted to. She was angry at the world. I don't think she ever grew out of this way of thinking."

"Caroline, that's understandable. It broke my heart when I had to come to your house and tell you Jeff was killed. Especially Kristen, she was so young. It's different now. Your lives are going to be getting back on track. It'll get better for you and her. All in good time, Caroline, just don't give up. I'll be here to help you and Kristen as long as it takes. I'm your friend, and I always will be," said Steve.

"That means a lot to me, Steve, to hear you say that. Kristen hasn't been this happy since before her dad died. After he died, she never smiled, and when she did, it wasn't that often. Well, should we make our entrance?" asked Caroline.

"Yes, let's go in," said Steve.

Caroline and Steve walked into the room and stood next to the wall, watching Kristen and Mike playing cards.

Kristen looked at Caroline and Steve after the game was over and said, "Mom, how did the meeting go?"

"It went all right. After the meeting Steve and I went to the ice cream shop to have an ice cream cone," said Caroline.

"Mom, guess what the doctors said. I get to go home soon. I'll still have to come here for therapy, but that won't be so bad. I beat Mike eight times at poker," said Kristen.

"Is that right, Mike? Well, don't feel bad. She beats me every time I play with her too," said Steve. Mike looked at Steve and grinned.

Mike stood up and gave Kristen a kiss on the forehead and said, "Well, Kristen, I would love to play another game with you. But unfortunately, my wife should be home from work. I want to talk to her before she goes to bed. Oh, by the way, I'm going to bring Janette with me tomorrow when I come to visit. If that's all right with Caroline and you," said Mike, looking at Caroline.

Caroline shook her head and said, "That sounds all right with me. I would love to meet your wife. If Kristen doesn't mind, I don't. What do you think, Princess? Are you up to meeting a new visitor?" asked Caroline.

"Yes, it would be nice to meet his wife," answered Kristen. Kristen looked at Mike who had a big smile on his face.

As Mike walked out of the room, he said, "Sounds great, so Janette and I will be here tomorrow. She'll be so happy tonight when I tell her. We'll see you all tomorrow when we get here then. Good night."

"Well, Caroline, I had a lovely evening, but I guess I should get going too. Four thirty in the morning comes quick. Kristen, I'll see you and Caroline tomorrow after work," said Steve.

"Steve, be careful when you're at work," said Caroline.

"Mom's right, please be careful at work," said Kristen.

Steve looked at Caroline and Kristen, who looked concerned. He walked over to Kristen and gave her a kiss on her forehead and said jokingly, "Don't worry. You can't get rid of me that easily."

Kristen looked at Steve who was grinning. She started smiling and looked at Caroline standing next to Steve. Caroline had a huge smile on her face. Steve turned to look at Caroline. Then he gave her a hug. "Remember what I told you earlier. I'll be here for you and Kristen as long as it takes. I promise," said Steve as he left.

For a couple of minutes after Steve left, it was quiet. Then Kristen said, "Mom, he's such a nice person. I hope we see a lot of Steve Telly. He makes me laugh, and his partner Mike does too."

"I hope we do too, Princess. He is a real caring person," said Caroline.

Caroline continued getting help for her drinking. She went to Alcoholics Anonymous meetings regularly. Kristen was in the hospital for another few days. It was quite a struggle for her to get her body functions back to normal. It took weeks of therapy. On the day Kristen was released from the hospital, Steve, Caroline, Mike, and Janette planned a welcome-home party for Kristen. It wasn't a big one, but Caroline had talked to Cheyenne and Sasha's parents to see if they could be there. Cheyenne and Sasha were given permission to go to the party.

Mike Mitchell picked the girls up while Caroline and Janette were at Caroline's house getting the house ready. Steve went to the hospital and picked up Kristen. When Steve and Kristen got there, Caroline turned the lights down. Steve walked in first, and when Kristen came in and closed the door, she turned around and saw her best friends standing there smiling at her. She saw a sign hanging on the wall. It read, "Welcome home our little princess!" Janette, Mike, Steve, and her mom were standing in the back of the girls. Kristen almost cried because she was so happy. She gave everybody a hug.

Kristen went back to school and started getting good grades. Steve stopped over to see Caroline and Kristen quite often. Once a week, he took them out to eat. Caroline and Kristen got a second chance at happiness. Officer Telly helped Kristen and Caroline get past this and helped Caroline move on with her life. He started caring a lot for Kristen and her mother. Officer Telly went to Alcoholics Anonymous meetings with Caroline often. Six months later, they became best friends and started going out together. Two months later, Caroline was told she had ovarian cancer. The doctor told her that they caught it early enough, so they would have a better chance of getting rid of it. The doctors got her started on chemotherapy right away. Two weeks after Caroline started chemotherapy, she started getting nauseous and tired more than usual. Caroline started getting a cold. She was coughing a lot. Steve was getting concerned about Caroline. She was getting to the point she couldn't keep hardly any food down. One month later, she started getting sicker.

It was a Monday morning, Kristen got ready for school and came downstairs to eat breakfast when she saw her mom lying on the couch. "Mom, you don't look so good. Do you want me to stay home? I can go to school and talk to them. They could give me my homework, and I could come back home," asked Kristen.

"No, Princess, I feel fine. I don't want you to miss school. I'm okay, sweetie," answered Caroline. Caroline didn't want Kristen to know how she was really feeling. Caroline just wanted to sleep.

"Are you sure, Mom? It won't be any trouble. I'll take care of you," asked Kristen.

"Yes, Princess, I am sure. I'm just going to lie down for a while. Go to school, sweetie. I'll see you when you get home," answered Caroline. Kristen looked at her mom worried. Then she gave her mom a kiss on her forehead. Then she went to school.

When Kristen got home from school, her mom was still lying on the couch. Kristen started talking to her mom, but there was no response from her.

"Mom, talk to me please," said Kristen. There was still no response. Kristen checked her mother's pulse. Her pulse was very weak, and she wasn't breathing right. Kristen ran to the phone and called 911. Then she called the police station to get a hold of Steve, but Steve had left earlier to get a gift for Kristen and Caroline. Mike picked up the phone when he heard it was an emergency phone call for Steve and that it was from Kristen.

"Kristen, what's wrong? Steve left early to pick something up for you and your mom. What's going on?" asked Mike.

"It's Mom. She wasn't feeling good when I went to school this morning. I offered to stay home, but she told me she didn't want me to miss school. When I got home, I was talking to her. She wasn't responding, so I checked her pulse the way we learned in school. Mom's pulse was very weak, and she was breathing funny. She won't wake up."

"Kristen, did you call 911?" asked Mike.

"Yes, but I need to talk to Steve to help me. I don't know what to do. I don't want to lose my mom," said Kristen.

"Don't worry, Kristen, I know where Steve went. I'll go and get him. We'll be there as soon as possible. I have to go, goodbye," said Mike.

Mike told Captain Flynn what had happened. The captain told him to hurry and find Steve. When Mike arrived at the mall where Steve had gone to, he walked up to the information booth. He asked them to page Steve Telly. Five minutes later, Steve walked up to the information booth. He saw Mike standing there pacing.

"Mike, what's going on? What happened?" asked Steve.

"It's Caroline. We have to go. Caroline is sick and won't wake up. Kristen called me. I told her we would be there as soon as possible. I'll explain it all on the way to the hospital.

"We'll leave your car here and pick it up later," explained Mike.

When Mike was talking to him, Steve felt numb. They quickly left the mall. On their way to Caroline's, Mike filled him in on what was going on. Steve's heart felt like it was being torn out. Minutes later, they pulled into the driveway. An ambulance was there, and the back doors of the ambulance were open. They were bringing Caroline out of the front door. The paramedics had her hooked up to a heart monitor. They quickly put her in the ambulance. Kristen followed the paramedics. Kristen ran up to Steve when she saw him.

"Steve, can I ride with my mom? Please?" asked Kristen.

"Mike, Kristen needs to ride with you. Can you follow the ambulance?" asked Steve.

"Yes, we'll be right behind you," said Mike.

"Don't worry, Kristen. Caroline will be okay. I'll be with her. I don't want you to be there in case something happens. You're like a daughter I never had. It's not for your eyes. They might have to do something that could make you sick. Trust me, Princess. I know what I'm doing. I won't let anything happen to your mother. I love her as much as you do," said Steve.

Just then, he realized this was the first time he admitted to Kristen he loved Caroline. Steve realized what he had said to Kristen, so he quickly looked at her to see how she had responded. Her eyes lit up when she heard what Steve said. Kristen smiled at Steve and then got in Mike's car. Steve jumped into the ambulance and asked the paramedics how Caroline was doing. The paramedics told him it was going to be touch-and-go because the chemotherapy had weakened her immune system. She'd contracted pneumonia.

"Her left kidney is starting to shut down. We have to hurry," yelled the paramedics.

Steve just looked at Caroline and started praying, "Please, God, don't let Caroline die. Kristen and I need her." At that moment, Steve realized how Jeff felt fifteen years ago when Caroline went into premature labor. Steve was a rookie cop then, and he hadn't known how to help Jeff or Caroline who was lying motionless on the floor. Steve felt as helpless as Jeff did. When the ambulance got to the hospital, the paramedics rushed Caroline through the glass doors. Steve followed the paramedics to the room where they took Caroline.

Steve's eyes started tearing, and he felt like the world was caving in around him. He watched the doctors working on Caroline through the glass windows of the room. Suddenly a nurse closed the drapes. Steve stood there frustrated.

Mike and Kristen pulled up next to the ambulance and parked. They got out of the car and ran through the glass doors. They asked the nurse where Caroline was. When they arrived, they saw Steve just standing there. He looked dazed and lost. Kristen looked at him with worry.

Mike knew that look on Steve's face all too well. It meant bad news.

"Steve, how is Caroline? Were there some problems on the way here?" asked Mike.

"It's not good. On the way here, her left kidney started shutting down. The doctors are working on her now. Mike, what happens if I never get to tell Caroline how much I love her? She'll never know how much I really love her," said Steve.

"Don't worry, Steve. You'll get to tell her. And besides, Caroline knows how much you care about her, doesn't she, Kristen?" said Mike.

Kristen stood there, stunned over how Steve was acting. She didn't know he cared so much about her mom. Kristen smiled and said, "Mike is right. Mom knows you care about her. She cares a lot about you too." Hugging Steve, Kristen said, "Mom won't leave us. She's stronger than we think she is. Mom is just tired, and she needs rest. You and she didn't give up on me when I was in a coma. We're not going to give up on my mom. My dad won't let her leave us. Just like he wouldn't let me die," said Kristen. Mike had tears in his eyes when Kristen said that to Steve.

"Kristen's right, Steve. Faith is going to bring her back to us. Love doesn't die that easily. I'm going to call Janette. She and Caroline have become good friends, and Janette would want to be here for Caroline. I'll be back," said Mike.

When Mike got back, Steve and Kristen were sitting in the chairs in the hall. Mike sat next to Kristen and asked Steve if anyone came out to talk to them yet. Steve shook his head no. Kristen and Steve both looked so lost and dazed. Mike wasn't sure what to say to Steve and Kristen. He just sat there staring at the clock, hoping someone would come out and talk to them about Caroline's condition.

Meanwhile, in the room, Caroline was lying motionless. She started having a vision, and in the vision, there was a tunnel. Caroline walked through the tunnel. At the end of the tunnel, there was a beautiful, bright, sky-blue light. Jeff stood at the end of the tunnel in the light. When Caroline got to the end of the tunnel, she looked at Jeff. Jeff looked like he did the last time Caroline saw him. Jeff looked at Caroline and said, "Hello, my gorgeous queen, how is Half-pint?"

"Kristen is doing great, Jeff. Why am I here, Jeff? Am I dead?" asked Caroline.

"No, but if you don't go back, you could die. I'm here to tell you it is not yet your time. Caroline, you have to go back. Half-pint needs you, and so does Steve. He really loves you and our Half-pint. You can't leave our little Half-pint alone. Half-pint would be traumatized if she lost both her parents. She can't take another parent dying. Steve loves you as I do. He wouldn't know how to live without you. He would die inside like you did when I died. Caroline, I want you to be happy. You have to live. They both need you so much. I love you, and I'll miss you when you go back. But I'll see you again someday. It was nice seeing Half-pint when she was in the hospital. I told her the same thing. It wasn't her time. I love you, my gorgeous queen. I'm proud of the way you've turned your life around. Steve is a lot like me. He is a good man, and I trust him to take care of you and Kristen. Tell Half-pint I'm proud of her, and I love her. Now you have to go before it's too late Caroline," said Jeff.

Caroline's eyes were tearing as she looked at Jeff. Tears rolled down her cheeks, and she hugged Jeff and kissed him goodbye saying, "Goodbye, Jeff, I'll always love you."

"I know, my queen, but don't let that get in the way of your happiness with Steve. Steve is good for you and Half-pint. Be happy, my gorgeous queen. I will always love you, Caroline. Goodbye," said Jeff. Caroline walked back into the tunnel, crying as she walked. When she turned around to look at Jeff, Jeff had tears in his eyes. Then he disappeared.

Steve and Kristen waited to hear some news about how Caroline was. Janette showed up a half hour later. She walked up to Kristen and hugged her. Then she asked, "Mike, is there any news on Caroline?"

"No, nobody has come out of the room yet to let us know," answered Mike.

"Kristen, don't worry. Your mom is a strong woman. She'll pull through this with flying colors," said Janette.

Steve just sat in the chair quietly and listened. Finally the doctor came out of the room and asked, "Are you people here for Caroline Winters?"

"Yes, we're here for Caroline Winters. How is she?" asked Steve.

"Well, it was touch-and-go for a while, but we managed to get her finally stabilized. We're sorry we weren't out here sooner to talk to you. You can go in and see her now, only one at a time though. She's not very coherent yet. Caroline was severely dehydrated. We almost lost her, but I think there will be a good chance she'll pull through. She'll probably be here for a week or two until she's better," said the doctor.

Steve looked at the doctor and then at Kristen and said, "Kristen, you should go in and see Caroline first."

"Steve, you should go in first. I think mom needs to hear how much you care about her. Then after you get done talking to mom, I'll go in and visit," Kristen said, smiling.

"Are you sure, Kristen?" asked Steve.

"Yes, I'm sure, Steve," answered Kristen.

Steve walked into the room and saw Caroline lying motionless in the hospital bed. "Please, Caroline, don't die on me and Kristen. Caroline, Kristen and I love you so much. I don't know what I would do without you. What about Kristen? What would happen to Kristen? Caroline, you and Kristen have come quite a long way. It's going to get better, I promise. You've just got to have patience. You have to keep fighting. Well, I have to go. The doctor only wanted one person in here at a time. Your little princess is waiting to come in. I'll come back later. Please don't give up, Caroline," begged Steve as his eyes teared.

Steve went out in the hall and told Kristen she could go in. When Kristen went in, Steve started to talk to Mike and Janette.

"Mike, Kristen is going to be home alone until Caroline comes home. I can't let her stay home by herself."

"No, we can't let that happen, Steve. That is why Janette and I planned on taking her home with us until Caroline goes home. We know when you're not at work, you'll be here with Caroline. Janette will bring Kristen here to visit Caroline every day after school. Don't worry, Steve. We got it covered. That's if you don't mind," said Mike.

"What would I do without my best friends? That will help a lot. Thank you," said Steve.

Shortly after they got done talking, Kristen came out of the room. She sat in the middle of Steve and Mike.

"Kristen, Mike and Janette would like you to stay with them until your mom gets better. Janette will bring you here to visit your mom every day after school. What do you think? Would that be all right?" asked Steve.

"Yes, I guess. But what happens if mom needs me, and I'm not here? What about you, Steve? Are you going to be with my mom?" asked Kristen.

"Don't worry, Kristen. Your mom is very strong. The nurses will be checking on her really often," said Janette.

"Kristen, I'll be here when I'm not at work. I'll be fine. Mike and Janette will take good care of you. Your mom will be able to recover better knowing you're being taken good care of."

It was getting late; so Janette, Mike, and Kristen left. Kristen had to get up early to go to school. Janette wanted Kristen to get her homework done before she went to bed. On their way home, they stopped at Kristen's house to get her homework and some clothes. Before Kristen went to bed, she, Mike, and Janette played a game of poker.

Steve spent the night at the hospital with Caroline. In the morning, at four, Caroline awakened, and she stared at Steve who was sleeping. Steve had his chair right next to the bed, and his head was on the bed next to her hand as he slept. Caroline moved her hand and brushed through his hair with her fingers and said, "Steve, where is Kristen? Please wake up and talk to me."

Steve heard Caroline talking to him, so he quickly opened his eyes. "Caroline, you're awake. We were so worried about you. Kristen is staying with Mike and Janette until you get to go home," said Steve, giving her a kiss and a gentle hug.

"Caroline, please don't ever scare me like that again. Kristen and I thought we were going to lose you," said Steve.

"Steve, did you mean it when you said you loved me?" asked Caroline.

"I meant every word I said, especially when I said I love you," answered Steve.

"Good, because I was hoping I wasn't dreaming," said Caroline smiling. "Steve, why am I in the hospital? What happened?"

"You were brought in last night to the emergency room. Honey, you were barely breathing when you got here. You almost died on Kristen and me. You have to hurry and get better so I can take you and Kristen to my parent's ranch, okay, Caroline?" said Steve.

"Steve, I'm kind of groggy and kind of tired," said Caroline.

"That's because of what you went through last night. You need your rest, gorgeous. Kristen will be here after school to see you. Why don't you close your eyes and rest. I have to go to work. Please don't forget, I do love you, Caroline. I'll come and visit you during my lunch break. Mike will be with me," said Steve. Leaning, he gave Caroline another kiss and said, "See you later, gorgeous."

At lunchtime, Steve and Mike came to see Caroline. She slept until they arrived. After he left, she fell asleep. Caroline started getting a fever. Her condition was getting worse again. The doctors tried everything they could to bring the fever down. Instead, it went higher. When Janette brought Kristen to see her mom, the doctors restricted the visit. Janette called Mike at work and told him Caroline's condition was worsening. Caroline had a fever, and it was climbing. Mike said, "How can that be? She seemed better when Steve and I were there at noon. I'd better tell Steve. I dread telling him. We'll be there as soon as we're done here. I have to go, Janette. We'll see you in a little bit."

Mike went to find Steve. Steve was standing by the drinking fountain when Mike found him. He told him that Caroline was getting worse. Steve was so upset he didn't know what to say. He was speechless, stunned, and dazed. Captain Flynn looked at Steve when he walked past. He saw the look on his face, pulled Mike to the side, and said, "Mitchell, what's wrong? Why does Steve look like he lost his best friend?"

"Captain, Caroline is getting worse. She's burning up with a fever. The doctors tried everything to bring it down. Nothing is working. I just told Steve that Janette just called and told me this," answered Mike.

"Oh no, I thought you said she was getting better. Well, sometimes a person thinks the patient is getting better. But in fact, they're getting worse. I was hoping she was getting better," said Captain Flynn. "Mitchell, I don't want him to drive. He is in no shape to drive. Why don't you drive him to the hospital? You can leave now. You and Telly are the best officers on the force. I don't want Telly working when he has so much on his mind. He needs a clear head when he has this kind of job to do, or something could go wrong. I heard you're taking care of Kristen. Is that true?" said Captain Flynn.

"Yes, Janette and I took her home with us last night," said Mike.

"That was a good idea. At least Telly won't have to worry about Kristen being by herself. Feel free to bring her here if Janette has to work. We'll give her a tour of the police station, and she can see where Telly and you work. It would be nice to have a young one hanging out here again. My son is all grown up, and he doesn't stop to see me that often. How old is Kristen?" asked Flynn.

"Kristen just turned sixteen last month. She's a really smart kid too. She's really good at card games. She beat the pants off of me when she was in the hospital, and we played poker," said Mike.

"Good, bring some cards with you when you bring her here. There is nothing better than a good game of poker. I'll be looking forward to playing cards with her," said Captain Flynn.

Mike and the captain walked over to Steve who was standing next to the wall. Steve's eyes were bloodshot from tears.

"Telly, I want you to go to Caroline. You shouldn't be here. She needs you. Mitchell told me what's going on. I understand what you're going through. My wife went through something similar to what Caroline is going through. Caroline is strong just like her dad and mom were," said Captain Flynn.

"What? Do you know about Caroline's parents? Where are they? Caroline never talked about her parents," asked Steve.

"Yes, her father was my best friend. He and his wife are at the Hills Cemetery. Caroline never knew her parents. Her parents were killed in a car accident on their way back from a seminar. Nathan and Kristy had to go to it for work. Catharine and I were taking care of Caroline until they got back. Nathan and Kristy never made it back to my house. If Caroline would've been with them, she could've died too. Caroline was only nine months old. After her parents died, I and the missus tried to adopt Caroline because she had no kin left. But the state took her from us and put her in a foster home. They said the kind of job I have would not be stable enough. I thought they were wrong, but I was a rookie cop at that time. I've been keeping tabs on how she's been doing since the state took her from us. The moral of me telling you this, Telly, is through everything, Caroline has always made it through obstacles thrown her way. She'll get better," said Flynn.

"Why didn't you tell me that you knew Caroline?" asked Steve.

"Telly, you never asked. If you would have, I would've told you long ago. I want you to take a couple of days off, and stay with Caroline. I'll take two vacation days from your vacation time so you still get paid for those days. I'll have Brooks cover for you while you're gone. I want you to take care of Caroline, but I want you to make a promise to me," said Flynn.

"What promise, Captain?" asked Steve.

"I want you to promise me when Caroline gets better, you'll invite me and the missus to the wedding. Catharine and I would love to be there for you and Caroline," said Flynn.

Steve smiled and said, "I promise you. You'll be the first to be invited to our wedding."

"Good, Mitchell will be taking you to the hospital now. I'll see you in two days. That's an order Telly. I and the missus will be praying for you and for Caroline to get better. Now get going. Caroline needs you," said Flynn, patting Steve on the shoulder as he walked away smiling.

Mike and Steve left as soon as they grabbed their clean clothes out of their lockers. When they got to the hospital, Kristen was sitting in the hall crying. Steve walked up to Kristen, hugged her, and said, "Your mom is going to be all right, Princess. Don't worry. She's been through worse things than this, like the time she went into premature labor the day you were born. We almost lost you and your mom that day," said Steve.

"Steve, how do you know about that? Did mom tell you?" asked Kristen.

"No, Princess, I was there. I was the officer that got the call. I was a rookie cop back then. I wasn't that experienced yet. I just thank God you and Caroline survived that ordeal. Otherwise, we wouldn't be standing here having this conversation. Would it bother you if I asked your mom to marry me? I would never try to replace your dad. I really care about you and your mom," said Steve.

"I would be happy if you and mom got married. Then I would be able to call you dad instead of Steve. My mom loves you too. I see it in her eyes whenever you're around. I haven't seen mom happy like this since before my dad died. I approve of mom being with you. You're the best thing that has happened to her. I think of you as a father already," said Kristen smiling.

"I think of you as my daughter, Kristen. In my eyes, you and your mom are my family," said Steve grinning.

Steve hugged Kristen and said, "Well, Princess, we'll be a family soon when your mom gets better. I promise. Has a doctor come to talk to you and Janette?"

"Not yet. We're still waiting for them to come and tell us how Mom is," answered Kristen.

Mike and Janette followed Kristen and Steve to the waiting room. They sat down and started reading magazines displayed on the coffee table. Fifteen minutes passed Steve started getting nervous as they waited for a doctor to come in to tell them how Caroline was. He got up and walked out into the hall. He saw a doctor coming out of Caroline's room, so he stopped him.

"Doctor, how is Caroline? Have you been able to bring the fever down?" asked Steve.

"No, we haven't been able to bring the fever down. Everything we've tried has been unsuccessful. We're running out of ideas. You're Officer Telly, aren't you?" asked the doctor.

"Yes, you can call me Steve," said Steve.

"I've seen you here before. That's how I knew your name. Steve, do you believe in God?" asked the doctor.

"Yes, I do strongly, why?" asked Steve.

"Because I think you should go to the chapel and pray. We've done everything we can to help Caroline. Nothing seems to work. Only God can help her now. I'm on my way to the chapel if you want to come with me. Caroline needs as many people praying for her as possible. We need a miracle. It doesn't look too good right now. I'm sorry," said the doctor.

Steve looked at the doctor and his eyes started tearing. "Is it really that bad doctor?" he asked.

"Yes, I'm afraid to say it, but it is. God is the only one I know who can help her get better. All we can do is have faith in our Creator, hoping he'll help her. There is a good chance Caroline won't survive this," said the doctor.

Steve suddenly got depressed, thinking of how he had to tell Kristen that her mother might not recover. He went to the chapel with the doctor to pray for Caroline. After they both got done praying, they walked back to Caroline's room.

"Doctor, could I go in to see Caroline?" asked Steve.

"Yes, you can. She needs as much encouragement as possible, Steve. You can call me Craig," said the doctor.

Steve went in to see Caroline. He sat in the chair next to her bed and moved it up closer to the bed. Steve picked up her lifeless hand.

"Caroline, you can't leave us now. We need you. Can you hear me? You have to keep fighting. The doctors have done what they can. It's up to you now and our Creator. Don't let the pneumonia win, gorgeous. I'll be with you for the next two days, Caroline. My boss gave me some time off so I could be with you. I found out my captain knew your parents. Captain Flynn said he would pray for you. He also said you need me more right now. He's right. He knew your parents, Caroline. And the sooner you get better, the sooner he can tell you about them," said Steve hoarsely as tears fell down his cheeks.

Mike wondered where Steve had gone, so he told Janette and Kristen he would go look for him. Mike went up to the window and looked into Caroline's room. He saw Steve crying.

"Steve, are you okay?" asked Mike.

"I talked to the doctor. He told me there was nothing else they could do for Caroline. Mike, you and Janette have to take Kristen to the chapel to pray for Caroline. The doctor told me only God could help her now," said Steve.

"Oh my god. Is it that bad, Steve? Are you sure?" asked Mike.

"Yes, it is that bad. We need a miracle, Mike," said Steve.

Mike put his hand on Steve's shoulder and said, "Don't worry, we'll go right now." He left the room and talked to Janette and Kristen. He took them to the chapel. Kristen sat in the back pew.

"God, please don't let my mom die. Daddy, don't let Mom die. I know you're watching over us. You have to help Mom. She's getting worse instead of better. Mom finally has someone who really cares for her. Steve loves us. Bring her back to us. Please talk to God," said Kristen as she prayed.

After they were done praying, Mike and Janette went back to the waiting room. Kristen went into Caroline's room. Steve was sitting next to Caroline's bed, holding her hand. Kristen looked at Steve whose eyes were bloodshot from crying.

"Steve, Mom and I are very lucky to have somebody like you who cares about us. Don't worry. Dad won't let her leave us. He knows we need her," said Kristen.

"Princess, I'm lucky to have you guys in my life. It has to get better. There is so much I have planned for you and your mom. I want to take Caroline and you to meet my parents. They live on a ranch in Kentucky. They have over one thousand acres of land. I was going to take Caroline and you on one of the horse trails," said Steve.

"Steve, I've never ridden a horse in my life," said Kristen.

"That's okay. I was going to teach you how to ride. It's not that hard to learn. My parents are really nice. I've told them so much about you and Caroline," said Steve.

"It sounds like fun. We still can go there. We'll just have to wait until Mom gets better, that's all. Can we take her when she gets out of the hospital?" asked Kristen.

"I never thought of that. Yes, we could take her there the weekend after she gets out, if she feels up to it. It's quiet and peaceful, and it would help her feel better. That's a good idea, Princess," answered Steve.

Steve walked over to Kristen and gave her a bear hug. Then he sat back down. Kristen grabbed the chair on the opposite side that Steve was on. She held her mom's hand, and Steve held Caroline's other hand. They sat there staring at Caroline. For the longest time, it was quiet until Mike came in there to see how Steve and Kristen were doing.

"Steve, Janette is going down to the cafeteria. Do you or Kristen need anything?" asked Mike.

"I think it's going to be a long night, Mike. It probably wouldn't hurt to get some coffee and soup. It doesn't matter what kind it is.

I'll eat whatever you bring back. What about you, Kristen? What do you want?" asked Steve.

"I just want some milk. Thank you," said Kristen.

"Steve, will you be here with Mom after Janette, Mike, and I leave tonight?" asked Kristen.

"Yes, I'm going to stay overnight so I'm here if your mom wakes up. I'll be off the next two days, so I'll be here pretty much all the time. Don't worry, Kristen. I won't be leaving. I'll be here with your mom," said Steve.

Those two days were the longest days Steve ever had. Caroline was so pale and weak from the fever. On Steve's second day off, Caroline's fever broke. Steve was exhausted from not getting enough sleep. Every time he heard a noise, he woke up and looked at Caroline to make sure she was all right. When Mike, Janette, and Kristen got to the hospital, they looked into the window of Caroline's room. Steve looked tired and exhausted. He looked like he was going to pass out. They entered the room.

"Steve, you need to get some rest. You're not helping Caroline by getting run-down. When Caroline wakes up, don't you want to look well rested? If she sees dark circles under your eyes, she'll worry about you. Go home, and get some sleep and a change of clothes. Caroline's fever is going down now, so hopefully she'll wake up soon. If she does wake up before you get back, we'll tell her you had to go home and will be back as soon as you can. I'll stay here until you get back," said Mike.

"Mike is right, Steve. Mom wouldn't want you to get run-down over her being in the hospital. Please go get some sleep. Mom would want you to take care of yourself," said Kristen.

"Yes, I guess you guys are right. I'll go home and get some sleep. If anything happens, call me, okay, Mike?" said Steve, getting out of the chair.

Steve walked over to Kristen and gave her a hug. Then he walked over to Caroline's bed, kissed her on the forehead, and said, "See you later, gorgeous. I'll be back later. I love you, Caroline." Grabbing his jacket, he left.

Steve went home to get some sleep. Three hours later, he came back. "Steve, did you get enough sleep?" asked Mike.

"Yes, I slept pretty good. Has Caroline awakened yet?" asked Steve.

"No, she hasn't. Steve, I called the captain and told him how Caroline was doing," said Mike.

"That was a good idea, Mike. He's been really worried about Caroline too," said Steve.

"Mike, where is Princess?"

"Janette had to take her home. It was getting late, and Kristen needed to do her homework. Kristen wrote you a note before she left. She told me not to forget to give it to you," said Mike. He handed Steve the letter.

Steve opened the letter, and it read, "Steve, it would be nice to see you and Mom get married. Please be with Mom. She needs your strength and love. If my mom awakens while I'm gone, tell her I'll see her after school and that I love her. Love ya, Kristen. PS. I can't wait until the day I can call you dad. You'll be a cool dad."

Steve's eyes started watering, and tears rolled down his cheeks when he read the letter. Mike had a grin on his face. Kristen let him read the letter when she wrote it.

"Mike, how can I be so lucky to have such loving people in my life, like Caroline and Kristen?" said Steve.

"Well, it wasn't luck, Steve. It was fate. Fate is what brought them into your life. Yes, you're very lucky to have them," said Mike.

Steve shook his head in agreement. He walked over to the chair and sat down next to Caroline.

"Mike, you should go home and get some sleep. I'll see you at work tomorrow. Tell my little princess I loved the letter." Mike agreed and left. Around ten o'clock, Caroline awakened. When Steve saw her open her eyes, he grinned.

"Good evening, gorgeous. It's about time you woke up. I thought I wasn't going to get to talk to you before I had to go to sleep. I have to go back to work tomorrow. At least I can see those beautiful baby blue eyes of yours. Now I know I'll sleep well," said Steve, grinning at Caroline.

"Steve, I just saw you at noon," said Caroline.

"Caroline, it's been two days since you've been unconscious. You were burning up with a fever for that long. The fever broke earlier today," said Steve.

"Really? I'm going to miss your company when you go back to work tomorrow, Steve," said Caroline.

"Don't worry. At lunchtime, I'll be coming here to see you, gorgeous. By the time you get out of here, you'll want to get away to a ranch in Kentucky, my parent's ranch. They want to meet my future wife. I called them after Kristen and I talked. Kristen and I thought it would be a good idea after you get better. The day you get out of the hospital, we're going to go to Kentucky for the weekend. That is if you feel up to it. I promised Kristen I would teach her how to ride horses. What do you think, Caroline?" asked Steve.

"Yes, I think that is a great idea. It'll be nice to get away for a while," said Caroline.

"Caroline, Captain Flynn knew your parents. He can tell you a lot about your mom and dad. Your dad was his best friend. If you were with your parents, you could've died too. Captain Flynn told me a lot. Maybe if you ask him, he might have some pictures he could give you," said Steve.

"It would be nice to show Kristen a picture of her grandparents. It would be nice to see what they looked like. I always wondered what my real parents were like," said Caroline.

"In time, you'll find out. But right now, you need to get some rest. I'll wake you up before I leave for work, gorgeous. So try to get some sleep, Caroline," said Steve.

Caroline looked at Steve and smiled. Then she closed her eyes and fell asleep. Steve fell asleep around eleven. At four in the morning, Steve woke up. He talked to Caroline for a while, and Caroline asked him to ask Captain Flynn for the pictures of her parents. Steve told her he would ask him when he got to work. He left to go home and get ready for work. Caroline's condition was improving. When Steve got to work, the captain was in his office. Steve filled his coffee cup and put creamer and a teaspoon of sugar. He went to his desk and sat down. Shortly after, the captain came up to his desk.

"It is nice to have you back, Telly. I'm so glad Caroline is doing better. Catharine and I are going to go and see her after I get home from work, so don't be surprised if you see us at the hospital," said Flynn grinning.

"Captain, are you going to tell Caroline what you know about her parents? Do you have any pictures of her parents?" asked Steve.

"Telly, the missus and I made an album out of all the pictures we had of her parents. We made it for Caroline. We held on to it for years, hoping someday we could give it to her. We were thinking of bringing it to Caroline tonight, so she and Kristen could look at it together. It's going to be our get-well present. What do you think, Telly? Is it too soon to give it to her?" asked Flynn.

"No, Caroline and I were talking this morning before I came to work about how she wanted to know what her parents were like. I told her you knew her parents. She wanted to talk to you," said Steve.

"Well, good I'll tell her everything she wants to know. I'm looking forward to tonight more than you'll know. We'll be talking about my best friend," said Flynn. The captain patted Steve on his shoulder and walked away smiling.

At noon, Steve and Mike went to see Caroline. Steve walked in first, and Mike followed. "Hi! Gorgeous, did you miss me?" asked Steve jokingly.

"Well, to be honest, I just woke up five minutes ago. But yes, it's nice to see you here. How is work going today?" asked Caroline, looking at Mike and Steve.

"Work is going great now that you're getting better. Caroline, you're going to have a visitor tonight, and you're going to benefit from this visit quite a bit. Make sure that you get plenty of rest, okay, gorgeous? Tonight a lot of questions will be answered," said Steve with a big grin on his face.

"I'll make sure I get plenty of rest then," said Caroline smiling

Steve talked to Caroline for a while until his break was over. Then he and Mike went back to work. Caroline went back to sleep.

After school, Kristen and Janette came to the hospital. Caroline was awake when they came into her room. Kristen looked at her mom with a smile on her face.

"Mom, thank God you're awake. How are you feeling?" asked Kristen.

"I feel much better. How is school going, Princess?" asked Caroline.

"It's going great. When I don't understand something, Janette and Mike explain it to me. They've been a big help. I prayed to Dad to help you," said Kristen.

"Kristen, when you were here in the hospital in a coma, did your dad visit you?" asked Caroline.

"Don't think I'm crazy, Mom, but yes, I was walking through this tunnel. At the end of the tunnel, Dad was standing in the light. I never told you because I was afraid you would think I was crazy," said Kristen.

"Well, Princess, if you're crazy, so am I because I experienced the same thing. I talked to your Dad. He told me he had talked to you when you were in the hospital. He told me to tell you he loves you and that he's proud of you. Jeff told me it wasn't my time to go. Jeff also told me he told you the same thing," said Caroline.

"So it really happened, Mom? It wasn't just a dream?" asked Kristen.

"No, Princess, it wasn't a dream. God works in mysterious ways. Your dad showed me the way back like he showed you the way back Kristen," said Caroline smiling.

Janette stood there listening, amazed at what they were talking about.

"You guys are so lucky to have experienced the light at the end of the tunnel like that. I heard about people having experienced the bright light and the tunnel. I never thought I would ever know anyone who had experienced it. Have you told Steve yet?" asked Janette.

Kristen and Caroline both looked at Janette smiling. "Janette I haven't talked to Steve yet about what happened. I wanted to talk to Kristen first to see if it really happened. I thought I was dreaming too," said Caroline.

"Yes, that makes sense. You wanted to make sure. I would've done the same thing," said Janette.

"Janette, thank you for taking care of my little princess while I'm here," said Caroline.

"You've become my best friend, Caroline. I enjoy Kristen's company. Anytime you need some time to yourself, all you have to do is call me. I'll be happy to have Kristen stay with us. Caroline, you don't have to worry about anything right now. I just want you to get better, okay?" said Janette.

They talked and laughed and had a good time. Around six thirty, Steve and Mike showed up. As they walked into Caroline's room, they saw the women laughing.

"Well, ladies, sounds like you're having fun without us," said Mike grinning.

"It's nice to see everybody laughing again, especially you, gorgeous," said Steve. His eyes lit up when he walked in, seeing everybody laughing.

"Well, Caroline, when are you and my partner getting married?" asked Mike.

Caroline looked at Steve and started blushing. Steve had a twinkle in his eyes when Mike asked her that question. Caroline was speechless.

Steve said, "When the time is right, only when Caroline decides that she is ready, not until." Steve looked at Caroline and the color of her face was turning back to the color it was supposed to be.

"Well, gorgeous, I'll be back. I'm going to get some coffee. Would you like something, Kristen? What about you, gorgeous? Do you want me to sneak something in here so you can have a treat?" asked Steve.

"No, I'm not really hungry, Steve. Thank you anyway," said Caroline.

"Steve, can you get me some milk?" asked Kristen.

"Anything for the two ladies in my life," answered Steve.

Steve left the room and went to the cafeteria. As he walked back to Caroline's room, he saw Captain Flynn and his wife Catharine walking toward Caroline's room. Captain Flynn and his wife saw Steve, so they stopped and waited for him. When Steve got next to them, they walked into Caroline's room together. Steve handed

Kristen her milk and then introduced the captain to Caroline and Kristen.

"Caroline, here are the visitors I was telling you about earlier. This is our captain. Caroline and Kristen, meet Captain Flynn and his wife Catharine," said Steve.

Kristen and Caroline smiled. "Nice to meet you, Mr. and Mrs. Flynn," said Kristen as she shook their hands and smiled.

Caroline looked at Steve and pulled him down to her so she could quietly ask him a question. "Steve, is he the one who knew my parents?" whispered Caroline.

"Yes, he's the one who knew your parents, gorgeous," said Steve.

Steve stood next to Caroline, and Kristen was on her other side. Janette and Mike were on the same side as Kristen. Captain Flynn and his wife were on the same side as Steve.

Caroline smiled, and her eyes lit up when Steve said they were the people who knew her parents. "It's quite a pleasure to meet you, Mr. and Mrs. Flynn," said Caroline.

"Telly, you forgot to tell me how beautiful they both were. Caroline, you have your father's eyes and so does Kristen. Ladies, I and the missus brought something that you and Kristen could both benefit from. Oh, by the way, you can call me Roy."

He looked at Catharine smiling and then at Caroline, who looked confused. Catharine handed Caroline the album. Caroline's eyes lit up. She looked at Roy and Catharine and asked, "Does this album have pictures of my parents in it?"

"Yes, we've waited a long time for you to come back in our lives, Caroline. Telly brought you back into our lives. This album will show you what your parents looked like. Catharine and I made this album for you. So if you ever came to us and asked us questions, about your parents Caroline, we would have this to give to you to help you understand who your parents were. Any questions you have, I and the missus will answer. All you have to do is ask us," said Roy.

Caroline opened the album. The first page had Roy and Catharine and her parents in it. Caroline's Dad had a police uniform on. Her mom and dad both had black hair. Her mom's eyes were brown, and her dad's eyes were blue. Caroline showed Kristen the picture.

Then Caroline asked Roy a question, "Roy, my father was a police officer?"

"Yes, he was, Caroline. He was my partner and best friend," answered Roy.

"Princess, look at this. Here's a picture of your grandma and grandpa," said Caroline.

Steve stood next to Caroline and stared at the picture. He was shocked to find out her dad was a cop. He had a huge smile on his face. Caroline had tears in her eyes. It was like finding her identity for the first time. For the first time, she knew what her parents looked like.

Mike, Janette, Catharine, and Roy watched Caroline, Steve, and Kristen as they looked through the album. They all stood there quietly.

After a few minutes went by, Kristen asked a question, "What are my grandparents' names?" She looked at Roy and Catharine.

"Your grandparents' names were Nathan and Kristy, Kristen," said Roy.

"Where are they?" asked Kristen.

"Nathan and Kristy were killed in a car accident. Kristen, your mother was only nine months old. Catharine and I were babysitting Caroline. Nathan had to take her to a seminar for Kristy's work. They never made it back to our house. We tried to adopt you, Caroline, but the state wouldn't let us. That's when we decided to put all the pictures in an album for you, hoping someday you would come back into our lives," said Roy.

"How old were my parents when they died, Roy?" asked Caroline.

"Nathan was thirty-one, and Kristy was twenty-eight. Caroline, your parents loved you so much. They were very protective of you. They hated not being able to take you with them. We should thank God that you weren't with them because if you had been with them, you could've died too," answered Roy.

"Where are my parents buried?" asked Caroline.

"They're buried at the Hills Cemetery. When you get out of the hospital, I and the missus will take you there. You need to concentrate on getting better right now so we can take you there, Caroline. We'll stop back another day when you get better. Right now, you need to get some rest," said Roy. He looked at Caroline. She looked exhausted. He walked up to Caroline and hugged her. Catharine smiled at Caroline and hugged her and then hugged Kristen.

"Caroline, it's nice to have you back in our lives. We missed you. You have such a beautiful daughter. She looks like you a lot," said Catharine as she walked toward the door.

"Oh, Kristen, I hear you can play a mean game of poker. I'm looking forward to playing cards with you one of these days. Have a good night everybody," said Roy as he hugged Kristen. As Catharine and Roy left the room, they both were smiling.

"Well, Princess, it is getting late. You should get going to do your homework. I love you, Princess. I'll see you tomorrow. I'm feeling really tired," said Caroline.

"Mom, I love you too. Get some rest, and don't worry about me," said Kristen as she hugged her mom.

"Yes, it is getting late, ladies. Caroline, you're right. We should get going, so you can get some rest. Steve will take good care of you, Caroline. Good night," said Mike.

Mike hugged Caroline and said, "Take care of my partner. Keep him in line, okay?"

Janette hugged Caroline and said, "Caroline, Kristen and I will see you tomorrow. Don't worry. I'll make sure Kristen stays caught up on her homework."

"Steve, take care of my best friend," said Janette.

As Mike, Janette, and Kristen left, Steve shut the door to Caroline's room so it would be quieter. "Well, gorgeous, it looks like it's just you and me now," said Steve.

"Steve, I can't believe Roy and Catharine gave me this album full of pictures of my parents. I'm afraid to go to sleep because I'm afraid when I wake up tomorrow, the album will be gone. I might be dreaming all of this. I don't want this to be a dream," said Caroline.

"Well, gorgeous, it's not a dream. Tomorrow when you wake up, this album will be here for you to go through again. Caroline, I had no idea your father was a cop, nor did I know he was Captain Flynn's partner years ago. Your parents sound like they were really loving people. You have a lot of them in you. When Captain Flynn was telling us about them tonight, I realized you have a lot of the same special qualities about you. That's what made me fall in love with you," said Steve.

"You have some special qualities about you too, Steve. You're a loving, caring person. You're funny, handsome, and sensitive. That's what made me fall in love with you. I can't imagine what life would be like without you. I love you, Steven Telly," said Caroline.

Steve kissed her on the forehead and leaned on the bed. Putting his arms around her, he said, "Caroline, I wish I could have you in my arms all of the time, twenty-four hours a day would be nice. It feels so right."

"You're right, Steve. It does feel right," said Caroline.

Steve sat there for the longest time. He kept his arms around Caroline. When she fell asleep in his arms, he just watched her until the nurse came in to check on her. The nurse came in. She smiled. Steve stood up and grinned.

"How is she? When can I take Caroline home?" asked Steve.

"Sir, at the rate she's going, she'll be getting out sooner than we thought. If she keeps getting better, she shouldn't be here too long. It's nice to see you care so much about her. A lot of TLC is what makes a person get well faster. We want to get her started back on chemotherapy as soon as she gets strong enough. Ovarian cancer is one of the worst cancers for women. A lot of women die from this cancer because they don't catch it early enough. The chemotherapy is helping her. There is a good chance we can kill the cancer. The sooner we get Caroline back on chemotherapy, the sooner we can get it under control. I'm glad the doctor caught it before it got worse. You two look good together, and your daughter is so polite. Whenever I come in here to check on your wife, your daughter talks to me. She's a good kid," said the nurse.

Steve stood there with a big grin on his face. He didn't want to embarrass the nurse by telling her they weren't married. He decided not to mention it. "Yes, I am lucky to have such a special, loving family," said Steve. He didn't say anything else. In Steve's eyes, they were a family.

After the nurse left, Steve sat in the chair next to Caroline's bed. He laid his head down by her hand and fell asleep. At four thirty in the morning, Steve woke up. Caroline was still sleeping. He got up and stretched, and then he woke Caroline up by kissing her on the cheek.

"Morning, gorgeous, I have to get going. I'll be thinking of you when I'm at work. See you later, gorgeous," said Steve.

Caroline looked at the table next to her bed. There on the table sat the album. "Steve, it wasn't a dream. It really happened. I have pictures of my parents," said Caroline.

Steve looked at Caroline and smiled. "No, you weren't dreaming, gorgeous. It really happened. A lot of questions were answered last night. I'll see you after work, gorgeous. Keep getting better, my sweets," said Steve. He hugged her and kissed her on the forehead. Walking toward the door, he stopped when he heard Caroline talking to him.

"Steve, be careful at work. I love you, Steve," said Caroline.

"I'll be careful because I have a beautiful woman waiting for me when I get done," said Steve as he left.

When Steve got to work, Captain Flynn was waiting for him at Steve's desk. When Captain Flynn saw Steve, he was smiling.

"Telly, how is Caroline?" asked Roy.

"She's making a speedy recovery. When Caroline is strong enough, they're going to start her on chemotherapy again. They're pretty positive about a full recovery from the pneumonia and the ovarian cancer. They feel that the chemotherapy is working. I hope they're right. I can't imagine life without Caroline. I want to thank you for giving Caroline the album. She is so happy. When Caroline is happy, I'm happy. Captain you and Catharine will have to come over for dinner when Caroline gets home. She really likes you and your wife. You two made quite an impression on her and Kristen," said Steve.

"I and the missus would love that. I'll tell her what you said, Telly. She'll be so happy, just like me. When Caroline gets out of the hospital, she's going to need a lot of rest. She shouldn't be home alone. I and the missus are worried about that," said Roy.

"I know, Captain. That was worrying me too until Kristen came up with a good idea. When Caroline gets out of the hospital, I'm going to take her and Kristen to Kentucky for the weekend. It's only an hour's drive, to my mom and dad's ranch. I promised Kristen I would teach her how to ride a horse. It's nice, quiet, and a beautiful place for Kristen and Caroline to relax and not worry about anything. When we get back from Kentucky, I'm going to ask Caroline and Kristen to stay with me until Caroline fully recovers," said Steve.

"Steve, Catharine could stay with Caroline until Kristen gets home from school every day. She wanted me to ask you if she could. Catharine and I love Caroline so much. We've missed watching her grow up. This would give Catharine a chance to get to know Caroline better. Her heart is set on helping Caroline. Catharine and I were heartbroken when the state took her from us.

"We promised ourselves if Caroline came back in our lives, we would never let her walk out again. We missed her growing up. We don't want to miss anything else," said Roy.

"Captain, tell Catharine that's an excellent idea. I think Caroline would love the idea of getting to know you and Catharine more. You're the only connection she has to her parents," said Steve. Captain Flynn patted Steve's shoulder as he walked away smiling.

When Kristen and Janette got to the hospital, they went to Caroline's room. Caroline was looking at the pictures in the album.

"Mom, how are you feeling today? Can I look at the pictures of Grandma and Grandpa again?" asked Kristen.

"Yes, Princess, you sure can. I'm feeling well rested. In a few days, the doctor is going to start me on chemotherapy again," said Caroline.

"Mom, did Steve spend the night here with you?" asked Kristen.

"Yes, Steve stayed here last night. Seeing as how I'm getting better, I'm going to tell Steve to go home tonight. He looked uncomfortable last night sleeping on this chair. I want him to get a good night's rest," said Caroline.

"We're so happy that you are getting better. We can tell how much Steve cares for you. We can also tell how much you care about Steve too, Caroline. Mike and I have never seen Steve so happy," said Janette.

Caroline, Kristen, and Janette talked for about two hours until a florist came in with a bouquet of roses.

"I'm looking for a Mrs. Winters. I was told this was the room to go to," said the man.

"I'm Mrs. Winters. Who are they from?" asked Caroline.

"They're from a Steven Telly," said the man. The man handed Caroline the bouquet of roses. There were eleven red roses and one white rose in the middle. The bouquet held baby's breath and two ferns and was displayed in a white frosted crystal vase. Caroline looked at the flowers and put them on the table next to her bed. Kristen and Janette were smiling. Kristen walked up to the bouquet and smelled the roses. She noticed a card was hidden in the middle of the bouquet next to the white rose.

"Mom, there's a card next to the white rose," said Kristen. She grabbed it and handed it to her mom.

Caroline pulled the card out of the envelope and read it. It read, "To the most beautiful woman that ever walked into my life. I'll never stop thinking of you gorgeous, no matter where I am."

Caroline's eyes started tearing. She handed Kristen the card. Kristen read it and gave her mom a bear hug and said, "See, I'm not the only one who cares about you. Steve cares for you too."

"Kristen is right, Caroline. He really cares about you," said Janette.

When Steve and Mike came into the room about an hour later, Kristen ran up to Steve and hugged him. After Kristen hugged Steve, he walked over to Caroline.

"Hi, gorgeous. I see you got the flowers I sent you. I've picked something else up for you. I wasn't going to give it to the florist. I wanted to give this to you myself," said Steve.

Mike, Janette, and Kristen stood there listening and smiling. Steve pulled out a box wrapped in rose paper out from his inside jacket pocket. He handed the box to Caroline. She looked at Steve and said, "Steve, the bouquet of roses would've been enough. You didn't have to get me anything else."

Steve smiled at Caroline and watched her as she unwrapped the box. When she opened the box, there was a necklace inside with three diamonds on a pendant. Her eyes popped wide open. She looked at Steve and said, "Steve, it's beautiful."

"Caroline, each diamond represents a person. One represents you, one represents me, and one represents Kristen. I consider us a family," said Steve. Tears of joy rolled down Caroline's face.

By the next week, Caroline was making a speedy recovery. The doctors resumed her chemotherapy. The doctor prescribed a pill to help her body rebuild its immune system. The drug was called Taxol.

Kristen and Janette came to visit Caroline every day after school, and Steve came to visit her after work. Finally it was time for Caroline to go home. Steve and Kristen came to pick her up.

"Well, gorgeous, are you ready to head for Kentucky?" asked Steve.

"Yes, I really am looking forward to this little trip. I'm looking forward to meeting your parents Steve," said Caroline.

Kristen stood smiling, amused by her mom and Steve. Steve pushed Caroline in the wheelchair while Kristen followed.

After leaving the hospital, they stopped at Steve's house. Janette had lunch ready for all of them. She wanted Caroline to have a home-cooked meal before they left. Captain Flynn and his wife were invited too. When Caroline, Steve, and Kristen arrived at Steve's house, Captain Flynn and Catharine were sitting on the couch. Steve walked in first, followed by Kristen, and Caroline was the last one to come in. Janette stood behind the door waiting for Caroline to close the door. When Caroline turned around, she saw Catharine and Roy get off of the couch and walk toward her. She turned around and looked at Janette who was holding a cake. Roy and Catharine hugged Caroline.

"Welcome home, Caroline. We were looking forward to this all week. It's so nice to see you out of the hospital. Steve tells us you're going to his parents' ranch after you eat. I and the missus got you a present to take with you. We figured you might get bored being away from home. Kristen told us you used to paint. So we got some canvas, paint, and the brushes," said Roy.

"Thank you, Roy and Catharine. I'll paint you a picture while I'm there," said Caroline.

"You don't have to do that, dear. We don't expect that," said Catharine.

Caroline looked at the cake Janette was holding. It was covered with frosted roses. "Janette, that's a beautiful cake," said Caroline.

"Thank you, Mike and I picked it out for you," said Janette.

They all walked to the table and sat down. Kristen sat next to Roy and Catharine. Caroline sat next to Steve who was at the end of the table. Mike and Janette sat next to Caroline.

Janette quickly went into the kitchen to get the chicken she'd baked. Caroline went into the kitchen to help Janette.

"Janette, do you need any help?" asked Caroline.

"No, Caroline, thanks for asking. Catharine came earlier to help get everything ready. She's been a big help, she and Roy. Caroline, you should go sit down. I don't want you to exhaust yourself. You have a long trip ahead of you. It will be worth it once you guys get there. We wanted you to have a home-cooked meal before you left for Kentucky. Catharine made the seven-layer salad. And Steve, being quite a cook, he made the bread," said Janette.

Caroline went back to the living room and sat down. Steve kissed her on the forehead and said, "Gorgeous, you're supposed to relax and not worry about anything. If Janette needs any help, I'll help her."

Caroline looked at Steve and smiled. Everybody talked until Janette brought the chicken to the table.

"Steve, could you cut the chicken up so I can go get the salad and bread?" asked Janette.

"Yes, I sure can," said Steve.

Janette went back into the kitchen to get the other food. When she sat down, they said a prayer and then ate. Afterward, Janette started taking dirty dishes off the table. Mike helped her carry the dishes to the kitchen, and he put them next to the sink. After the table was cleared off, Mike filled the sink up with water, and Steve and Roy came to give Mike a hand. The men told the women to sit down and visit. Mike washed, Roy dried, and Steve put the dishes in the cupboards. After they were finished, they sat by their wives and talked. Steve sat next to Caroline and Kristen. Steve realized it was getting late, so he told everybody they were going to get going. He wanted to get to the ranch before dark. Everybody gave Kristen and Caroline a hug.

"Mike, can you lock up when you leave? You guys can stay as long as you want," said Steve.

"Yes, I can lock up. Don't worry. I have it covered. Have a good weekend."

"Thanks, Mike. I appreciate this," said Steve.

Steve looked at the captain and Catharine and said, "Thank you for coming to visit Caroline and Kristen before we left."

"Thank you for inviting us. It meant a lot to us to be here. Catharine and I are going to help Mitchell get this place picked up before we head out. Telly, take good care of Caroline and tell your mom and dad hi for me. Tell them I and the missus will be coming up to visit next week. Have a good weekend," said Roy.

"We will have a great weekend. I'll talk to Caroline while we're there about Catharine staying with Caroline until Kristen gets home from school. My parents will be happy to see you and Catharine next week. Thank you for getting Caroline the painting supplies. That will help her keep her mind off the cancer. Lately I've noticed she has started thinking it isn't going to go away. This might be what she needs to bring her spirits back up," said Steve.

Caroline was standing by the couch where Mike, Catharine, Janette, and Kristen were sitting. Kristen got up and walked over to Steve and Roy.

"Mr. Flynn, are you going to give my mom away when Steve and mom get married?" asked Kristen.

Mr. Flynn looked at Kristen, stunned. He didn't know what to say. Steve almost cracked up laughing because he had never seen the captain speechless like that. Roy looked at Kristen and at Steve. Steve broke the silence and said, "Captain, that is a great idea. You're the closest thing Caroline has to a dad. I know Caroline would want it that way. Catharine could be one of the matrons of honor. What do you think? Do you want to be at our wedding?"

The captain looked at Steve and then at Kristen and said, "I would be honored to participate in the wedding. When are you and Caroline going to tie the knot?"

"I'm going to be taking them to Walt Disney World for vacation. Kristen and I are working it out right now. We're going to surprise Caroline. When we get there, I'm going to ask Caroline to marry me. Kristen asked me to wait until then. She wanted her mom's wedding to be perfect, and so do I. That means you and Catharine will have to fly to Florida the night before the wedding. We're going to stay there for one week, and then I'm taking Caroline to Las Vegas for our honeymoon. Can you fly to Florida, Captain?" asked Steve.

"I and the misses were going to go on vacation sometime. That sounds like a good time to go. We'll be there. You can count on us. I'll have to have somebody cover for Mitchell for a few days too. I can't see him flying to Florida one day and having to fly back home the next day. I assume Kristen is going home with Mike and Janette?" said Roy.

"Yes, she's going home with Mike and Janette."

"Catharine will be so happy when she finds out we're going to be at the wedding," said Roy.

Caroline was watching Roy and Steve talking with Kristen. She hugged Janette, Mike, and Catharine and said, "Thank you so much for helping me." They all smiled as Caroline walked away. Caroline walked up to Steve, Roy, and Kristen. They quickly stopped talking. They didn't want her to hear what they were talking about.

"Are we going to get going soon, Steve?" asked Caroline.

"Yes, we are. We want to get there before dark. Captain, I'll talk to you later. Well, ladies, should we get going?" asked Steve.

Caroline hugged Roy and followed Steve and Kristen out the door smiling.

When they got to the ranch Steve's dad was outside working on his 3010 John Deere tractor. Caroline and Kristen followed Steve as he walked over to his dad. Steve gave his dad a big bear hug and said, "Dad, how are you and Mom doing? Sorry, we're so late getting here. Do you need any help? I want you to meet Caroline and Kristen. Can you stop for a minute?"

Joseph Telly turned around and grabbed the towel that lay on top of a tire. "Are these the ladies you can't stop thinking about? Son, you didn't tell me how beautiful they were. Lucky for me, Roy called a few days ago and told me. Otherwise, I might have had a heart attack from the shock of the beauty," said Joseph jokingly. He looked at Caroline and Kristen, grabbed them both, and hugged them.

"Welcome to Telly Ranch. Caroline, how are you feeling today?" asked Joseph.

Caroline looked amazed at how Steve looked so much like his dad. "Thank you for having us here. Your ranch is beautiful. Kristen and I have been looking forward to coming. We'll try not to be too much trouble," said Caroline.

"Trouble? You could never be trouble. I could tell you some good stories about my son of him getting into trouble. He was quite a wild one when he was growing up. I thought he would never grow out of it. He surprised me. This time, when I finally think I got him figured out, he pulls one on me, and I realize I don't have him figured out at all. He's a great son. We brought him up right," said Joseph.

Caroline and Kristen laughed over what Steve's dad was saying because Steve started blushing. They walked to the house talking and went inside.

"June, we have visitors. Honey, come out and meet our guest for the weekend," said Joseph.

June hurried out of the kitchen, ran up to Steve, and hugged him, saying, "We were wondering if you had changed your mind about coming here, Steven. We thought you would be here right after you picked Caroline up from the hospital. We were getting worried. Your dad went outside to work on the tractor so he could get it off his mind. You, Caroline, and Kristen must be hungry," said June.

"Mom, I'm sorry it took so long, but Janette wanted Caroline to have a home-cooked meal before we got on the road. Roy and Catharine were there too. They wanted to see Caroline and Kristen before we left. We ate an hour ago, so we're still kind of full. We didn't mean to make you guys worry like that. Next time, I'll call if we get detained, okay?" said Steve.

"That sounds like a deal, son. We're glad you're here. We've been excited to meet Caroline and Kristen. Roy and Catharine called the night they went to the hospital to meet Caroline and Kristen. They were very excited and happy. They called us when they got back from the hospital. They said Caroline and Kristen looked so much like Nathan and Kristy, and they obviously were right. They do look like them a lot. We always wondered if we would get to see her again. Caroline, we were friends with your parents too. We weren't as close to them as Roy and Catharine though. Nathan and Kristy came here with Roy and Catharine quite a bit on weekends. Your mom would take her painting supplies up on top of the hill behind the house and paint beautiful pictures. We have a couple of Kristy's paintings hanging up in the living room. Roy and Catharine have a couple too. Ask them to show you them when you go over to their house. Do you want to see them Caroline and Kristen?" asked June.

Caroline looked at Steve who was grinning. Steve nodded his head once to let her know it would be a good idea and said, "I'll grab the bags out of the Jeep Cherokee. I always wondered who painted those pictures in the living room. I had no idea that your mother painted them. Your mother was a very talented artist, Caroline. Go and look at how beautiful they are."

Caroline and Kristen followed June to the living room. In the living room, where there was a lighted painting over the fireplace, the painting covered most of the wall. It was a picture of the ranch. The sky held the beautiful colors of the sunrise. The other painting was a picture of a field with a forest on both sides. The clouds looked like cotton puffs. Caroline and Kristen looked at them for the longest time.

"Mom, Grandma's signature is on it, look," said Kristen.

"Yes you're right, it is. Grandma was very talented, wasn't she, Princess?" said Caroline.

Kristen nodded her head and said, "Yes, I wish we could have known them. Grandma and Grandpa seemed unique."

"If you could have met them, it would've hit you harder when they died. Don't worry, we can help you understand Nathan and Kristy a little bit. They were loving people. I hear you used to paint too, Caroline. Roy and Catharine told me Kristen told them you did. Are you going to paint a little while you're here this weekend?" asked June.

"Yes, I might, but it has been quite a while since I last painted anything. I'm not as good as my mom. Could you show me the hill where she painted when she was here?" asked Caroline.

"Yes, I could take you to the very spot where she sat, tomorrow after lunch. It's so nice to have you here for the weekend," said June.

Steve went outside to help his dad fix the tractor. Kristen and Caroline visited with June. June took them on a tour of the house so they would know their way around. She showed them Steve's room and told them stories of when Steve was growing up. June also told Caroline and Kristen about the times when Nathan and Kristy were there. Steve was outside helping his dad fix the tractor.

"We'll be eating about six o'clock. So, Caroline, if you want to get some rest, you can. I'll wake you up when it's time to eat." Caroline started to feel exhausted, so she went upstairs to lie down. Kristen stayed downstairs and help June.

"Mrs. Telly, thank you for suggesting my mom get some rest. My mom looks exhausted. You have such a beautiful ranch, and I love how you got brick walls on both sides of the entrance. My mom has been excited about coming here to get away since Steve told her we were coming here. I can't wait until tomorrow. Steve is going to teach me how to ride horses. What kind of horses do you have?" asked Kristen.

"We have Arabians and Appaloosas. After supper, I'll take you to the barn and show you some colts. They need names. Maybe you and Caroline can help me name them. What do you think, Kristen? Are you interested?" said June.

Kristen smiled and said, "That sounds great."

Later when supper was ready, June went outside to tell Steve and Joseph the supper was ready. Kristen went upstairs to wake her mom up to tell her supper was ready. Caroline was feeling sick to her stomach.

"Princess, I don't feel the greatest. I'm too tired to eat," said Caroline.

"Don't worry, Mom. Stay in bed and rest. Steve or I will bring something up to you when you are able to eat. I love you, Mom," said Kristen as she hugged Caroline.

When Kristen came downstairs and went into the dining room, Steve and his parents were already sitting at the table waiting for Caroline and Kristen. Steve looked at Kristen, wondering why Caroline wasn't with her. Kristen had a worried look on her face. He quickly asked, "Princess, what's wrong? Where is Caroline? Is she coming down to eat?"

"Mom isn't feeling good, Steve. She isn't hungry. I'm worried. She looks so exhausted. Maybe the drive here was too much," said Kristen.

"Well, Kristen, the chemo is really hard on your mom. When the doctors kill the cancer, your mom will feel normal again. We have to pray the doctors can get rid of it. Until she gets better, her appetite won't be normal. I'll take something up to her later. I hear my mom is going to show you the colts after supper. She told me she is going to let you name them too. That sounds like fun," said Steve.

"How is the chemotherapy going for Caroline? Is it working?" asked Joseph.

"It seems to be working. The doctors told Kristen and me that we have to make sure she eats. If Caroline quits eating altogether, it could complicate things. It could be a negativity toward her recovery, but I think she's strong enough to get through this, with Kristen's and my help," said Steve. They ate supper, and then Kristen helped June wash and dry the dishes. Steve and his dad sat in the living room and played cards. After Kristen and June were done with the dishes, they went into the living room and sat down. They started playing cards with Steve and Joseph. Two hours later, June and Kristen went to the barn to see the colts. Joseph went out with them. Steve went upstairs to see how Caroline was doing. Caroline was sleeping when she heard someone open the door. She quickly opened her eyes. Steve stood in the doorway, looking at Caroline. When he saw Caroline open her eyes, he walked up to the bed and sat on the bed next to her.

"Gorgeous, how are you feeling? We missed you at supper. Kristen and my mom went outside to the barn. Honey, you have to keep eating, or you'll get sick again. I know you don't have much of an appetite, but you have to keep eating. Come downstairs and try to eat something please," said Steve.

"Steve, I wish I would start feeling better. I hate being so tired all the time," said Caroline.

"Don't worry, gorgeous. The chemotherapy is working. It is just going to take time for the doctors to get rid of the ovarian cancer. Caroline, when you were in the hospital—"

Caroline stopped him from talking by giving him a kiss, then said, "Steve, I want to talk to you about something that happened in the hospital. When I was in the hospital, I had a vision of a tunnel and a bright light. Jeff was standing at the end of the tunnel in the light. He talked to me and told me I couldn't die. He also told me he talked to Kristen when she was in the hospital. I asked Kristen about this. She had the same vision of Jeff and the tunnel and the bright light. I thought it was a dream, so did Kristen until I talked to her. It wasn't a dream. Jeff told us both it wasn't our time to die," said Caroline.

"Caroline, I believe you and Kristen. I believe he brought you and her back to me. I felt a presence with Kristen when she was in a coma and with you when you were being worked on in the ambulance. I didn't say anything because I thought I was imagining it.

"Being a cop, I've seen a lot of weird stuff. God works in mysterious ways. He sent Jeff to talk to you, so you or her wouldn't die before your time. Other people have experienced visions similar to yours. I'm glad he helped bring you two back to me. I don't ever want you or Kristen to forget Jeff. He'll always be welcomed into our conversation. I want you and her to be able to talk about him freely in front of me. I think it would be great to learn more about him.

"He'll always be a part of Kristen and your lives. I would never try to replace him. There is no way to replace a person. We're all unique in our own ways. You and Kristen are my family now, so is Jeff," said Steve as he hugged her.

Caroline looked at Steve smiling and said, "So you don't think I'm crazy?" asked Caroline.

"No, I think it was a miracle sent from God. You and Kristen are so lucky to have experienced such a unique experience. Not everybody is lucky enough to get to walk through the tunnel and live to talk about it. See, it proves that you two are special," said Steve.

"Thank you for understanding, Steve. I guess I'm getting kind of hungry. Let's go downstairs," said Caroline. Steve and Caroline went downstairs and sat in the living room after he made her a ham sandwich. Steve turned the television on and watched it with Caroline. Forty-five minutes later, Kristen came running into the house. She figured her mom and Steve were in the living room, so she went directly to the living room.

"Mom and Steve, you got to come outside to the barn. Mrs. Telly let me name the three colts, please," begged Kristen.

Steve looked at Caroline who had such a big smile on her face. Caroline stood up and asked Steve where their jackets were. Steve walked to the closet and grabbed Caroline's jacket and his. After they got their jackets on, then they headed for the barn. When they got in the barn, Kristen grabbed Steve's and Caroline's hands and dragged them to where the colts were. There was a pure-white colt, a dark-brown-with-black-mane colt, and pure-black colt.

"Mom and Steve, I named the white one Star, the black one Midnight, and the dark brown one Gemini. Aren't they beautiful? What do you think of the names?" asked Kristen.

"There beautiful names, it's almost like you were meant to name them," said Steve.

"Yes, you're right, Steve. Those names are perfect for the colts," said Caroline.

June and Joseph stood by Steve grinning. "Hey, Kristen, we have another horse that is going to be having a fowl soon. You pick such unique names we'd like you to name it when it is born. How about it? Will you name it?" asked June.

"Sure, I would love to. When is the horse going to have it?" asked Kristen.

"In five weeks. When she has it, I'll call you. Steve can bring you guys up here for another visit."

Steve, Caroline, Joseph, and June watched Kristen petting the colts. They talked and laughed and had fun. It started getting late, so they decided to go into the house. June and Joseph walked in front of Caroline, Steve, and Kristen. As Caroline, Steve, and Kristen followed Steve's parents, as they walked into the house, Steve said to Kristen, "After lunch tomorrow, we're going to go horseback riding, Kristen. We'll go down one of the trails. I'll take you down my favorite one first, Kristen," said Steve.

"That sounds great. Is Mom going with us?" asked Kristen.

"No, Princess, your mom is going to go on the hill where her mom used to paint," said Steve.

"He's right, Princess, I'm going to paint tomorrow. I want you to have fun while we're here, Princess, okay?" said Caroline.

"Well, I don't know about you, ladies, but I'm tired. I'm going to get some sleep. We got a busy day tomorrow," said Steve. Steve hugged Kristen and then hugged Caroline and gave her a kiss on her forehead and said, "Good night, ladies. I'll see you in the morning." Joseph was tired, so he went to bed too. June, Caroline, and Kristen weren't tired yet, so they stayed up and talked for a while in the living room. After a while, Kristen got tired, so she went to bed.

"Caroline, you make my son so happy. I have never seen him so happy. He really loves you. I see the twinkle in his eyes whenever you are around him. I was lucky to find that kind of love. Steve is a lot like his father. I can't wait until you become our daughter-in-law. Have you decided when you're going to tie the knot?" asked June.

"We really haven't discussed it yet. But we will, and when we do, I'll let you know. You are such a kind person. It would be nice to call you mom. I never got to know my real mom," said Caroline.

"I know, dear, but some things happen for a reason. Maybe if they wouldn't have gotten killed, something worse could've happened to all of you. There is always a reason for what happens. I know one thing your parents loved you so much. We are so glad you came back into our lives, Caroline, especially Roy and Catharine. They were torn when the state wouldn't let them adopt you. I don't think they ever got over it. Roy kept in touch with your foster parents for the longest time. But one day, they moved and out of the blue told Roy and Catharine it was a bad idea to keep in contact with them. All Roy and Catharine had was hope, hoping someday you would come looking for answers about your real parents. When you went to college, Roy didn't know where you were, not until you came back married to Jeff Winters. It was so hard for Catharine and him to stay away from you. One thing about Roy and Catharine is that they won't push themselves on anyone. I think they still see you as their baby. They can help you a lot when it is about your mom and dad, Caroline," said June.

Caroline and June stayed up until one o'clock in the morning. Then they both started getting tired, so they went to bed.

The next morning, Steve was up early. He helped his mom make breakfast. After the breakfast was made, he knocked on Kristen's door and said, "Rise and shine, Princess. Breakfast is ready." He then knocked on Caroline's door and opened the door. He walked over to the bed and said, "Gorgeous, breakfast is ready. Do you feel up to eating with us?" asked Steve.

"Yes, I actually feel well rested. I'll be down in five minutes," said Caroline.

"Good, that's just what I wanted to hear. You look beautiful in the mornings when you wake up. Well, gorgeous, I'll see you in a little bit then," said Steve as he kissed her on the cheek and went downstairs. Steve, June, and Joseph waited until Kristen and Caroline came downstairs. Then they all ate breakfast. After breakfast, Kristen and Caroline washed dishes for June. June showed them where everything went and said, "When you are here, it is your home too. Thank you too for doing the dishes, but you didn't have to do them."

"We know we didn't have to do them, but we wanted to do them. Didn't we, Kristen?" said Caroline.

Kristen was smiling and shook her head yes and then hugged June and said, "Mrs. Telly, we wanted to do the dishes for you because we like you. Just think if Steve and mom get married, we'll be family. I'll be able to call you Grandma. What do you think would I make an okay granddaughter?" asked Kristen.

"Yes, I would be the luckiest grandma in the world. I would be honored to have you call me grandma. You can call me that now if you want," said June smiling as happy tears ran down her cheeks. Caroline started feeling sick, so she went to bed to rest. Kristen and June went to the barn to see the colts. After lunch, Steve took Kristen horseback riding. Caroline and June went to the hill. On Sunday morning, they went to church. After they got back from church, Kristen asked Steve if he could take her on another trail. He told them after lunch, he would. After lunch, Steve and Kristen and Joseph went riding. June went up to the hill with Caroline and sat under the tree in the middle of the field. Caroline started her second painting.

June looked at her first painting and stared at it and said, "Caroline, you're a very talented artist. You should start painting more. You have the same gift your mother had. I'm so glad Steve found somebody special. For a while, we thought he would never find anyone. You are a wise choice. I can't wait until you become my daughter-in-law," said June. As the day went by, June realized it was starting to get late. She had to start getting supper ready.

"Caroline, you can keep this painting up in the room you slept in. Next time, Steve brings you and Kristen. You can finish it if you feel up to it. That will be your room when you are staying here. I wish this weekend wouldn't have gone so quickly. It seems like whenever we have fun, time goes too quickly," said June.

"June, do you think Roy and Catharine would like this painting?" asked Caroline.

"Yes, I'm sure they would love it. They'll be shocked at how beautiful it is," answered June.

Caroline hugged June saying, "Thank you for this wonderful weekend. Next time we're here, I'll finish the unfinished painting. That will be yours and Joseph's," said Caroline.

"Caroline, we'd be honored to have you're painting. You have a gift none of us have. That gift is like your mother's. You should be proud of that. That makes you one step closer to Kristy," said June.

Caroline grabbed her supplies and walked with June to the house. Steve and Kristen were playing cards in the living room. Joseph was watching them, amazed at how good Kristen was.

"Roy told me he was going to play cards with Kristen. Looks like he is going to have quite a challenge playing her. Roy has finally met his match," said Joseph laughing.

"Steven, are you guys going to stay for supper?" asked June.

"Yes, I suppose we could, but we have to get going right after. Mom, will that be okay?" said Steve.

"Yes, I think you should. Your dad will help me with the dishes later."

Caroline went upstairs to put the painting supplies and her unfinished painting in the room. "Oh, Mom, I was talking to dad about something. After we leave, he'll fill you in. You and dad are going on a little vacation," whispered Steve. June looked at Joseph who was smiling.

"Okay, I'll talk to him later. I have to get supper ready," said June.

They ate supper, and after supper; Steve grabbed Caroline's, Kristen's, and his bag. He put them in the Jeep. Steve hugged his parents and told them he loved them. Kristen and Caroline hugged them after Steve. Then they left to go back to Illinois. On the way home, Steve asked Caroline and Kristen to stay with him at his house until Caroline got better. He talked to her about Catharine. Caroline agreed to stay at Steve's house, and it would be a good idea to not be alone at the house while Kristen was at school. She loved the idea of Catharine staying with her during the day. Caroline wanted to know

Catharine and Roy more. That was one way she could get to know them more.

Monday morning, when Catharine came over, Caroline gave her the painting. Catharine had tears in her eyes and said, "Caroline, it is beautiful? Are you sure you want to give it away?" asked Catharine.

"Yes, I'm sure. I want you and Roy to have it. I really appreciate how you two have been helping me," said Caroline. The painting was a winter scene of the forest.

As weeks went by, Caroline started to feel normal. The chemotherapy was working. Three months later, during the summer, Officer Telly took Caroline and Kristen to Walt Disney World on vacation. During the vacation, he hired a plane to write the words, "Caroline, will you marry me?" in the sky. After the plane flew over, he got on his knees and handed her a small box wrapped in Tasmanian devil paper. Caroline unwrapped the box and opened it. Inside was a beautiful gold diamond ring. Caroline was stunned at first. She looked at Kristen who was staring at her mom, waiting for her to say yes. But her mom was so shocked she didn't know what to say at first.

"Mom, answer Steve. Do you love him? He loves us," said Kristen.

"Yes, I love him a lot, but what happens if he changes his mind?" asked Caroline.

"Excuse me, ladies. Let me answer that question. I will never change my mind, Caroline, because I've cared for you for a long time now. I can say I love you and mean it. It was Kristen's idea to ask you here on our vacation. I had planned on asking you before, but Kristen talked me into waiting until we were here. Well, Caroline, will you be my wife? Please say yes. I would be the luckiest man in the world if you would just say yes," said Steve.

Steve looked at Kristen, and Kristen looked at her mom and said, "Mom, he really loves you, and all Dad wanted for you was for you to be happy and be loved."

"Well, Steven Telly, if I'm to marry you, I need you to put this ring on my finger and make it official," answered Caroline. Officer Telly's eyes lit up with Caroline's answer.

Caroline handed him the ring. Steve carefully pushed the ring on her finger. Kristen stood watching with a big grin on her face. After her mom had the ring on, Kristen grabbed them both and hugged them.

"So, Dad, when are you and Mom going to get married? How about tomorrow?" asked Kristen.

"Well, Princess, it is up to your mom, hopefully sooner than later," answered Steve.

Steve and Kristen looked at Caroline with big smiles on their faces, waiting for a response. "Well, tomorrow sounds fine to me, but I'll need a dress. And we'll need witnesses. Who can be our witnesses?" asked Caroline.

"Well, Mike Mitchell, my partner, and his wife are flying here tonight, and Kristen and I have invited everybody already. They will all be here tonight so they don't miss the wedding. So, Mrs. Telly-to-be, you have nothing to worry about. Kristen and I have taken care of everything. Caroline, your dress should be arriving at the hotel shortly. Mike and his wife are bringing it with them. Kristen picked it out. You were with her and didn't even know it, my gorgeous wife-to-be," said Steve Telly.

Caroline was so happy her eyes were tearing. That night, when Mike and Janette Mitchell arrived, they went straight to Caroline's room to drop her wedding dress off. Janette stayed with Caroline to make sure it was the right size. Caroline tried it on and then came out of the bathroom to show Kristen and Janette.

"I love this dress. It's so beautiful. Kristen, when we were looking at wedding dresses, I didn't think you were paying attention. This was the only one that caught my eye. How did you get it without Steve seeing it?" asked Caroline.

"Janette and I went back to the store after Steve gave us the money to go get it. Mom, you look beautiful. It's like the dress was made for you. Steve is going to be shocked when he sees how beautiful you look," said Kristen.

"Kristen's right. Caroline, you look great. When Steve sees you in that dress, he'll wonder why he didn't marry you sooner. You're going to be a beautiful bride," Janette added.

"Thank you so much, Janette. I am so glad I got to meet you and become your friend," said Caroline.

"I feel so privileged to be your matron of honor. I'm glad Mike and I were given a chance to be a part of your wedding. We think so much of Kristen and you. We're so happy that you found someone who adores you both. He talks about you all the time at work according to Mike. The last two months he's been on cloud nine. It's funny because when Mike and I got married, he went through the same thing. I can tell you one thing, Caroline, we've got the best kind of men, the kind that will love us for who we are and not for what they want us to be. Steve was very lucky to find you. I see the love in your eyes whenever I bring up his name. Steve has the same love in his eyes whenever we bring up your name. It's so hard to find that kind of love," said Janette.

Caroline smiled and gave Janette a hug and then hugged Kristen and said, "Princess, you did well. I love you so much, and if your dad could see you now, he would be proud of you."

Caroline walked into the bathroom to change. Kristen and Janette started playing cards while Caroline changed. Caroline, Janette, and Kristen played cards for the rest of the night.

After Mike left Janette at Caroline's, he went to Steve's room and knocked on the door. Steve opened the door and said, "It's about time you got here. I thought I would have to have a drink alone to celebrate Caroline's answer. Here, have a drink. It's nonalcoholic beer. I don't want to have a headache on my wedding day. Besides, it's been a year since Caroline quit drinking. It's not fair for me to drink alcohol if she can't. That would be mean, don't you think, Mike?"

"Yes, you're right, Steve. You're going to have a lovely wife after tomorrow. There'll be no reason for you to work so late. You're going to have to get home to your pretty little wife so you can get some tender loving care," said Mike grinning. They talked for a while. Then it started getting late, so Mike told Steve to try and get some rest.

Mike stopped at Caroline's door and knocked. He could hear Janette giggling on the other side of the door. As Kristen opened the door, Mike walked in and said, "Ladies, it's kind of late. Don't you think you need your beauty sleep for the big day tomorrow? Janette, honey, you should let these beautiful ladies go so they can get some rest. Honey, I can't sleep without you. Please come with me to bed? It really is getting late," said Mike.

Janette looked at Caroline and Kristen. They did look rather tired, so she said, "Caroline, you do look extremely tired. We don't want you or Kristen falling asleep during the ceremony, and you should get some sleep. Mike and I should get some rest too. It's been a long day. I'll see you in the morning, okay?" As Janette and Mike walked out, they gave Kristen and Caroline a hug. Roy and Catharine were running behind schedule so they didn't get to the motel until late that night.

The following day, Steve brought Caroline a beautiful bouquet of white roses. Steve's mom and dad were there in the morning.

Caroline's wedding dress was a beautiful satin gown in soft peach. The shoulders were lined with a delicate peach lace. Her veil was made of soft peach tulle. Her bridal bouquet was white poms, baby's breath, and peach roses. Caroline and Steve got married in a lovely church that was over eighty years old. The church had angel statues and picture windows. The pews were decorated with white ribbons and white and peach lilies on each end. An elderly priest presided over the nuptials. Officer Mitchell was best man, and his wife was matron of honor. Roy gave Caroline away. Caroline became Mrs. Steven Telly.

After the ceremony, Steve looked at Caroline and said, "Well, Mrs. Telly, my gorgeous wife, we're going to go on our honeymoon in three days. In three days, we'll be on our way to Las Vegas for one whole week." Caroline's eyes opened really wide.

"Steve, what about Kristen? She starts school soon, and I promised her we would go shopping for some new clothes. We planned on going after we got back from our vacation," said Caroline looking confused.

"I know. Kristen told me, and I already talked to her. She said it could wait until you and I got back from our honeymoon. She wants us to relax and have fun. I asked Mike and Janette if they could take care of Kristen while we're on our honeymoon. Mike and Janette said they would love to have Kristen stay with them. They already planned out what they're going to do and where they are going to take Kristen. They've been excited about having her stay with them for the last three weeks. They don't have many guests over to their home. They told me it would be nice to have a teenager in their home again. It's been too long they said. So, gorgeous, don't worry about a thing," said Steve.

"You thought of everything, didn't you?" said Caroline.

"I didn't do this alone. Kristen helped me, so did Mike and Janette. I hope you were surprised, Caroline. We all wanted it to be perfect for you. Kristen and I love you so much," said Steve.

Kristen was standing next to her mom and her new dad grinning.

"I love you, Steve, and you too, my little princess, so much. This was like a dream come true," said Caroline, hugging Kristen and Steve.

Kristen was so happy and said, "I love you, Mom. And I love you too, Dad. I hope you guys have a great time on your honeymoon, and, Mom, don't worry about me. I'll be just fine. Mike and Janette are going to take me to see a movie when we get back home."

June, Catharine, Joseph, and Roy walked up and hugged Caroline, Steve, and Kristen.

"I have the most beautiful daughter-in-law and granddaughter. Don't you think, Roy?" asked Joseph.

"Indeed you do, Joseph," said Roy.

"Congratulations, Caroline and Telly," said Roy, shaking Steve's hand.

"Kristen, I and the missus would like to have you over to our house while your mom and dad are on their honeymoon. Joseph tells me I met my match playing cards with you. Would that be all right, Mitchell? Could you bring Kristen over to my house?" asked Roy.

"Yes, we can bring her over whenever you want us to," said Mike.

Caroline and Steve had fun on their honeymoon. When they got back, they gave Kristen, Mike, and Janette some presents. Kristen had a family with a lot of love in it again and a new dad, but she never forgot what her real dad said, "I'll always be watching over you and your mom and the man in the uniform." Now she understood whom her dad was talking about.

Caroline and Kristen moved into Steve's house. Caroline rented out her house. Later that year, the doctors told Caroline the cancer was in remission. They did tests on her to see if she could still have a baby. When the results came back, the doctors told her she was a lucky person because she could still have children if she wished. They took her off her medicines, and she was told to see a doctor once a year. They told her if she started to feel sick again, to come back immediately.

Two years later, on a Monday morning, Steve, in a hurry to get to work, forgot to put on his bulletproof vest before he left the house. Steve and Mike were called to the scene of an armed robbery in progress. Steve was shot, the bullet just missing his heart, by an inch.

Steve went into the grocery store first, and Mike followed. They walked in as quietly as they could. They heard the robber yelling at the cashier. They quietly crept up to where they had the suspect in sight.

"Give me the damn money, or I'll blow your brains out now!" screamed the suspect.

Steve looked at Mike and nodded his head, giving Mike the okay. They ran up behind the man. The man quickly turned and fired his gun. Steve was in the line of fire. He tried to dodge the bullet, but it was too late. Mike glanced at Steve, then back at the robber. The robber looked nervous and fired at Mike. Luckily the bullet missed him. Mike pulled the trigger aiming at the suspect's shoulder, then at the suspect's leg. The robber fell to the floor. Mike ran to Steve who was lying on the floor. Steve's shirt was soaked with blood. Mike called on the radio saying, "Officer Telly is down. We need an ambulance."

Captain Flynn was walking past the radio room when he heard Mike's call. He ran into the room and grabbed the receiver out of the dispatcher's hand. As the captain talked to Mike, the dispatcher called for ambulances. "Mitchell, how bad has Telly been hurt?" asked Flynn.

"We need two ambulances right away. The suspect has been shot too. It looks like minor injuries. Officer Telly's been shot, and it looks like the bullet might have gone near his heart. He's not responding. Hurry!" said Mike.

"Mitchell, backup is on their way. The ambulance is being called as we speak. I'll meet you at the hospital," said Flynn.

Captain Flynn ran out of the radio room and went to his office. He called Caroline and told her he was coming over to pick her up to take her to the hospital. He told Caroline Steve was shot. After he talked to Caroline, he called Catharine and told her to pick Kristen up after school and bring her to the hospital.

Meanwhile back at the grocery store, Mike had his hands over Steve's gunshot wound trying to slow down the bleeding. He was talking to Steve.

"Steve, hang on, buddy. Help is on the way. Think about Caroline and Kristen. You have to keep fighting to live for their sakes. They love you so much. They need you, Steve. You're my partner. You can't give up," said Mike.

When the paramedics arrived, they checked the suspect first. Then they asked Mike how bad his partner was. Mike told the paramedics Steve might have been shot near the heart, but he wasn't sure. When the paramedics heard that, one of the paramedics raced over to Steve. They looked at the wound, then looked at Mike and said, "This is really bad. We have to get him to the hospital as soon as possible, or we will lose him." They quickly put Steve in the ambulance. It seemed like it took forever to get to the hospital. When the ambulance got there, Steve was barely hanging on. His heart had stopped twice on the way to the hospital.

On the way to the hospital, Caroline asked the captain what the robber would be charged with. Captain Flynn told Caroline the robber would be facing twenty to fifty years in prison for attempted murder. When Caroline and Captain Flynn got to the hospital, they went to the emergency and Caroline filled out the consent forms. The nurse immediately took the papers to the doctors, who whisked Steve to the operating room to begin surgery.

Meanwhile, in the operating room, the doctors worked quickly on Steve, who was barely holding on. As they operated, Steve was having a flashback of Caroline and Kristen. It was when he went to their house to tell them Jeff had been killed. Darkness suddenly overtook him, and blackness engulfed him. Steve then started having a vision. He was walking in a tunnel. At the end of the tunnel, he saw someone standing in a beautiful bright sky-blue light. When he finally made it to the end of the tunnel, a man was standing there, staring at him. Steve thought the man looked familiar. He couldn't figure out who he was. Steve stood there for a while. Suddenly he remembered who the man was. Steve's eyes opened wider in shock at who was standing in front of him.

"Steve, I'm here to stop you from leaving Caroline and Kristen. You are all they have. My Half-pint would be crushed if you left them behind. I won't let you die this way. You make them so happy. Take care of my Half-pint and my gorgeous queen. I've told Kristen and Caroline it wasn't their time. I'm here to tell you the same thing. It isn't your time to go yet. I trust you, Steve. They're all I have. Besides, you're going to have new additions to your family soon. Promise me, you'll take good care of them," said Jeff.

Steve looked at Jeff and said, "You mean Caroline is pregnant? I promise you, I'll take good care of our family. Thank you for showing them the way back through the tunnel. Thank you for such a wonderful family and your help. But what about you Jeff?" asked Steve.

"It is time for me to go back to the heavens. My work is done. I'll be with you all in spirit. I'll be watching over you. You won't see me again until it is your time. When it is your time, I'll take you with me to the heavens. Now go and take care of our family," said Jeff.

Steve was in surgery for a long time; so Caroline, Captain Flynn, and Mike went to the hospital chapel to pray for him. Caroline began praying, "Jeff, if you can hear me, bring Steve back to us, please. Oh, God, don't let him die," begged Caroline. After they were done, Caroline, Captain Flynn, and Mike went to the waiting room. Mike was covered with Steve's blood, so Captain Flynn told him to go and try to get cleaned up. When Mike came back, Caroline and Captain

Flynn were sitting next to the television against the wall. Mike sat down next to Caroline.

"Have you heard anything yet, Captain?" asked Mike.

"No, it's too soon. It's only been twenty minutes, Mitchell," answered Flynn.

"Captain, I'd like to stay here, if I may, at least until we know how Steve is doing," said Mike.

"Don't worry, Mitchell. We're not leaving until we know how he is. Catharine is going to pick up Kristen and bring her here after school. Mitchell, why didn't Telly have his bulletproof vest on?" asked Flynn.

"Captain, this morning, Steve was running late. He forgot the vest at home. When we went into the grocery store, I forgot he didn't have one on until it was too late," answered Mike.

"Well, it's too late to yell at him. The damage is already done. He'll probably never forget it after this. He'll remember what happened when he didn't wear it," said Flynn.

Caroline stood listening to Mike and Captain Flynn talking. Then she became more worried. "Roy, Steve isn't going to get into trouble for not wearing his vest, is he?" asked Caroline.

"Don't worry, Caroline. I'm not going to say anything bad to him. I think he's learned his lesson. I'm just going to be straightforward with him. He shouldn't have taken such a big risk. I'm going to joke with him about it a little. The last thing he needs is an annoying boss. I want him to get better, not die on us," said Flynn grinning.

Caroline looked at Mike and then at Captain Flynn. They were both grinning. Caroline looked worried. Captain Flynn noticed Caroline biting her lip and knew she was worried.

"Caroline, don't worry. Telly is too stubborn and pigheaded to die. He's a strong person, and he'll get through this with few problems," said Flynn trying to get Caroline not to worry so much.

They waited and waited for someone to come out and tell them how Steve was. Finally, a nurse came out to talk to them, "Are you Mrs. Telly?"

"Yes, I am Mrs. Telly. How is my husband? When can I see him?" said Caroline.

"Your husband is still critical. The bullet just missed his heart. If it had been one inch higher, it would have hit his heart. Your husband is very lucky to be alive. One of the doctors will be out to see you in a few minutes, but he'll be brief because they want to do some tests. You won't be able to see him for another half hour. It is going to be touch-and-go for a while," said the nurse.

The nurse left the room. Roy, Mike, and Caroline waited until a doctor came out to talk to them. After the doctor came out, they went to the waiting room and sat there for a long time without talking. Roy left to call Joseph and June Telly to tell them what had happened. As he walked out, he gave Caroline a hug and said, "Don't worry, Caroline. he'll get through this. I'm going to call his mom and dad. You just stay here and try to relax."

Catharine called the school and told them that Kristen's dad was rushed to the hospital. She told the secretary she was going to come and get Kristen early.

When Roy got done talking to Joseph, the phone rang right after he hung up. Catharine was calling Roy on the cell phone, asking him to have Caroline call the school. Roy let Caroline use his cell phone after he called Steve's mom and dad. Caroline called the school and told them she needed Kristen at the hospital. Thirty minutes later, the nurse came back. Caroline, Roy, and Mike followed her to Steve's room. Caroline sat next to the bed. Steve didn't wake up until a half hour later. He had a heart monitor hooked up to him and an IV stuck in his arm. When Steve awakened, he looked at Caroline and Mike and Roy who were sitting on the other side of the bed.

"Hi, gorgeous, where am I?" asked Steve hoarsely.

"You're in the hospital, honey. You were shot," said Caroline.

Steve looked at Mike and Roy. He saw the blood on Mike's shirt. "Mike, are you okay? You aren't wearing my blood, are you?" asked Steve jokingly.

"Yes, I'm okay. And yes, this is your blood on my shirt. You shouldn't worry about me. You're the one who was hurt," said Mike.

"Captain, how did Caroline get here? Did you bring her?" asked Steve.

"Yes, I brought Caroline, Telly. You're lucky you didn't get yourself killed not wearing your bulletproof vest. I bet you'll never forget that heavy thing again, will you?" said Roy smiling.

"Captain, I think I've learned my lesson. I feel like I've been run over by a truck. I'll never forget that vest again. I'd rather be late than be on time without it," said Steve.

Steve looked pale as a ghost. Suddenly his heart monitor went off. Caroline stood next to the bed, crying. All Caroline could hear was "code blue" being called over the intercom. The doctors came running into Steve's room and told them to leave. Roy grabbed Caroline, and Mike followed. The doctors were working on Steve. Caroline felt so helpless. She stood in the hall feeling numb. Suddenly she collapsed. Roy caught her as she was falling.

"Mitchell, get some water, quick," yelled Roy.

Mike ran to get a cup of water and a doctor. Mike found a doctor and told him what had happened. The doctor knew whom Mike was talking about because he was the doctor who'd treated Caroline when she was in the hospital. When the doctor got to Caroline, she was still unconscious. Roy was trying to wake her up. The doctor asked Roy, "Is Caroline still taking the pills for the cancer? I need to check her. Help me get her into one of these rooms please."

"Doctor, Caroline's cancer went into remission six months ago. The doctors quit the chemotherapy. They said she didn't need it anymore," answered Roy.

They carried Caroline into the first empty room they could find. "Mitchell, stay by Steve's room in case a doctor comes out. I'll stay with Caroline," said Roy.

Mike stood in the hallway dazed. He was worried about his partner and about Caroline. She'd lost a lot of weight from her cancer treatments.

When Catharine picked Kristen up at school, she explained what happened to Steve. Catharine and Kristen got to the hospital in an hour. They saw Mike in the hall. Kristen ran up to him and hugged him. "Mike, how is Dad? Where is Mom?" asked Kristen.

"The doctors are working on Steve. Your mom collapsed, and a doctor is checking to see what's wrong. Roy is with Caroline," said Mike.

"Where are they. What room?" asked Catharine.

Mike pointed to the room. When they got into the room, the doctor was getting ready to take Caroline out. He was going to run some tests. Roy grabbed Kristen and Catharine and hugged them saying, "Don't worry, Kristen. Your mom and dad are going to be all right. The doctor is going to do some routine tests on Caroline."

"I'm going to stay with Caroline. Kristen, you stay with Roy and Mike, okay?" said Catharine.

Kristen nodded and walked with Roy over to Mike. They talked to help time go faster. The doctor came out and said they were going to move Steve to the intensive care unit and that Steve wouldn't wake up for a while. They waited in the hall for Catharine. When she came back, she brought Caroline with her. Catharine was smiling. Roy looked at Caroline, who looked tired.

"Caroline, are you okay? We were worried about you," said Roy.

"Yes, I'm fine. How is Steve? When can we see him?" asked Caroline.

"We can see him after he wakes up. They're keeping him in the intensive care unit on the third floor. We were waiting for you to get back. We wanted to go up to see him together," said Roy.

"Captain, can I use your cell phone to call Janette? I called her earlier, but she wasn't home," said Mike.

Roy handed Mike the phone and said, "Yes, here you go, Mitchell. Call her and have her come to the hospital. We'll meet you up in Telly's room, okay?"

When they got up to Steve's room, he was still unconscious though he had more color to his face. Caroline was on cloud nine from hearing the test results. Roy noticed Caroline was distracted since she and Catharine got back. "Caroline, is something wrong? You seem a little distracted," said Roy.

Caroline looked at Kristen who was standing next to Roy. "Kristen how would you feel if I told you, you were going to have a little brother or sister?" asked Caroline.

Kristen's eyes opened wide. She said, "I would say it was a miracle. I've been praying for this since you and Steve got married. I've always wanted a brother or a sister. But, Mom, won't it be risky?" asked Kristen.

"The doctor said a lot of women my age are getting pregnant. He said there would be just a slight risk. He said not to worry. I'm healthy now, so the risk would be small," said Caroline.

Roy looked at Catharine who was smiling. He grinned and said, "Catharine, is that why you were smiling when you and Caroline got back?"

"Yes, honey, isn't that great? Caroline asked if we would be the godparents when she found out. I told her we'd love to be the godparents to the baby," said Catharine.

Roy looked at Caroline, hugged her, and said, "We can't wait until the little one is born. You have to tell Steve so he has more reason to get better."

Roy looked at Kristen and said, "Kristen, you're going to be a big sister. What do you think of that? Looks like you got the miracle you've been praying for."

"I think it's great. I can't wait until the baby is born," said Kristen.

They waited for Steve to awaken. When he did, Roy, Kristen, and Catharine left the room so Caroline could tell Steve the news. "Honey, you have to get better. I want to tell you something," said Caroline looking at Steve.

He stared at her for the longest time. "Caroline, as long as our baby is healthy, I'll be happy," said Steve.

Caroline was stunned, wondering how Steve knew. "Steve, how did you know?" asked Caroline.

"Jeff told me when we talked. He told me we were going to have another addition to the family. That means you have to take it easy. I don't want you to overdo anything. Have you told Kristen yet?" asked Steve.

"Yes, I told her, and she is so excited. I also asked Roy and Catharine to be the godparents. You don't mind, do you?" asked Caroline.

"I think they're a good choice. They'll be good godparents to our child. Caroline, if it is a boy, I want to name him after Jeff. He helped me come back to you. Jeff told me to tell you he loves you and Half-pint," said Steve.

"Jeff would be a beautiful name for the baby, if it's a boy, Steve," said Caroline.

Caroline gently hugged Steve. When they finished talking, she went and told everybody to come in.

Mike waited for Janette to arrive so they could go to Steve's room together. They arrived shortly after.

Roy congratulated Steve and shook his hand saying, "Telly, it's about time you and Caroline have a little one. I and the missus are going to spoil that baby like we do Kristen. If you ever need someone to watch the baby, we'll do it. We'd like Kristen to come over too. That way, when the baby is sleeping, I can play cards with her. I'd like to win at least once or twice. One of these times, maybe she'll have mercy on me and won't beat the pants off me," said Roy jokingly. Steve looked at Roy grinning.

"Dad, you have to get better so you can go to my graduation in June too. After that, I can help Mom out more so she won't have to do so much. I'll wait until the baby is at least one year old before I go to college. I love you, Dad," said Kristen hugging him.

"I'm so lucky to have your mother and you in my life. I love you too, Princess. Are you sure you want to wait to go to college?" asked Steve.

"Yes, I want to spend some time with you and Mom and my new brother or sister before I go. I'm going to miss you guys a lot when I finally do go," said Kristen.

"We'll miss you too, Princess. Your little brother or sister will be lucky to have such a loving older sister. As they grow up, they'll need your guidance. I'm sure you'll be the best sister they could want. I'm proud of how you turned your life around, Princess," said Steve.

When Janette and Mike came, Kristen ran up and hugged them, saying, "Janette, Mom is pregnant. I'm going to have a brother or a sister."

Janette looked at Steve and Caroline and ran over to them and hugged them. "Congratulations, you guys. We've been wondering if you were pregnant after Mike told me Caroline fainted. I was hoping," said Janette.

"It's about time, you two have a little one, congratulations," said Mike.

They all talked and visited Steve and Caroline. It started to get late and Steve was getting tired and looking exhausted, so Roy and Catharine left. Mike and Janette took Kristen home with them, and Caroline stayed overnight.

The next morning, Joseph and June Telly arrived at the hospital. They walked into Steve's room and hugged him. Caroline was in the bathroom when they walked in. She was having morning sickness.

"Mom and Dad, I got a surprise for you. You're going to be grandparents. Caroline is pregnant," said Steve smiling.

They looked at him, stunned for just a minute. "Steven Telly, you better not be joking about this," said June.

"Mom, I'm not. I'm as serious as I can be. I'm going to be a daddy in six months, and you are going to be a grandma," said Steve.

June's eyes widened as she smiled. Joseph stood there grinning. "Well, son, I'm so proud of you and Caroline. You are going to be great parents. June and I are going to spoil our grandchild too," said Joseph.

"Dad, you and Mom are going to have to duke it out with Roy and Catharine. They want to spoil the baby too," said Steve jokingly.

"Well, why can't we all spoil it together?" said Joseph smiling.

"I suppose seeing as how you put it that way, you all could," said Steve.

"Where is the expectant mother?" asked Joseph.

"Caroline is having morning sickness as we speak. Just last week, she said she was feeling sick to her stomach. I was worried that the cancer might be back. Yesterday when I was brought into the emergency, Caroline fainted, so the doctor ran some tests on her. That's when we found out she was pregnant," said Steve.

As soon as Steve got done saying that, Caroline came out of the bathroom. Joseph turned quickly around and grabbed and hugged her. Caroline looked at Steve, who winked at her. She then knew he'd told them.

"Caroline, I heard you're going to have our first grandchild. God bless you. We've been hoping for one. You need anything, call us. We're going to stay here for a week or two so we can see that our only son and our beautiful daughter-in-law are feeling better," said Joseph.

"Joseph and June, where are you going to be staying? Do you need a place to stay?" asked Caroline.

"We're staying at Roy and Catharine's. We have friends taking care of the ranch while we're gone. We'll be visiting you and Steve here every day, if we can. Roy and Catharine are taking us out to eat after Roy gets home from work. We'll probably be here later on tonight too. Of course, we stopped here first to see you before going to their house," said Joseph.

June hugged Caroline. They talked for a while until Steve got tired. After Steve fell asleep, they hugged and kissed Caroline and left.

Roy, Catharine, Joseph, and June were at the hospital every night to visit Steve and Caroline who were staying at the hospital every night. While Steve was in the hospital, Mike and Janette came to the hospital every day with Kristen. Steve recovered fast. In a couple of weeks, the doctors let Steve go home. Roy made Steve take two more weeks off. When Steve went back to work, Roy put him on desk duty. He didn't want Steve out on the road until he was fully healed.

As months went by, Caroline's belly got bigger and bigger. She had regular checkups. Kristen helped out as much as she could so her mom didn't have to do a lot. Kristen was marking days off on the calendar as it got closer to her graduation. On the day of graduation, she got up early and made breakfast for her mom and dad. Roy and Catharine came over and helped Caroline decorate the house for the party. A little later, Mike and Janette arrived, and they helped too. Steve was at the mall getting Kristen's graduation present. After they finished, they sat down at the dining room table and talked.

"Roy, do you want to play cards?" asked Kristen.

Roy waited for everybody else to leave the room before he answered her, "Yes, that sounds like a good deal. Your dad should be getting back soon so I can talk to him and Mike together. Your dad and Mike don't know it yet, but they are getting promotions. And with Caroline pregnant, I think Steve will appreciate this promotion. He'll have more time to spend with Caroline, the baby, and you. It is a safer job too. With the baby coming, he'll need more time to spend with them and you before you go to college too. Mike and Janette will have more time to spend together as well. Everyone will benefit from this," whispered Roy.

Mike, Janette, Caroline, and Catharine were in the living room at this time. When Steve got home from the mall, Roy pulled him and Mike to the side and talked to them. He was making them detectives. Steve and Mike were so happy they'd passed the exam and made detectives.

After Kristen's graduation, they came back to the house. Kristen opened her graduation presents. Steve bought some CDs of bands she liked and a boom box CD player for her to take when she went to college. Roy and Catharine bought her a computer. Janette and Mike bought her a typewriter. Caroline gave her two sets of bedroom quilts and matching sheets and pillowcases to go with them. Everything she got she could use when she went to college. Steve's mom and dad bought Kristen a Pontiac Grand Am, so she would have a way to get to school. Everybody was so happy that Kristen was going to college. Before they left, they all told her if she ever needed help with books or anything, to give them a call.

The following week, Kristen took her mom to the clinic to have a sonogram. The doctor asked Caroline if she wanted to know what sex the baby was. Caroline told him no. She and Steve wanted to be surprised. Caroline did want to know if the baby was healthy. The doctor told Caroline she wasn't having just one baby. He told her she was having twins. The doctor told her the babies were healthy so far. Caroline and Kristen stopped at the precinct to talk to Steve. When Caroline told him she was having twins, Steve asked her about having Mike and Janette as the godparents to the other baby. Caroline thought that would be a great idea, so they walked over to Mike and asked him.

"Mike, we're having twins. We have a problem though. Only one of the babies has godparents. Caroline and I were wondering if you and Janette would be the godparents to the other baby," said Steve.

Mike was filled with joy inside and said, "Janette and I would love to be the godparents to the other baby."

Steve smiled at Mike and kissed Caroline and said, "Gorgeous, I'm going to call Mom and Dad to tell them we're having twins. They'll be so happy when they find out we're having twins. They might go a little overboard on buying things for the babies. Gorgeous, my mom and dad do spend a lot of money on gifts. But let them, if they want to. When they bought Kristen the car for a graduation present, I didn't say anything to them because it would hurt their feelings. I've learned over the years you don't try and stop them from doing what they want.

"The car they bought for Kristen didn't even put a dent in their wallet. You and Kristen are family. They love you two so much. If we had tried to stop them from buying that car for Kristen, their feelings might have been hurt. My parents are that way. Family means everything to them," said Steve.

Weeks went by, and Kristen took Caroline to the clinic whenever she had to go for checkups. In her seventh month, Caroline started cramping. Kristen took her to the clinic to make sure nothing was wrong. The doctor told Caroline bed rest was what she needed to do. The babies seemed fine, but the doctor didn't want to take any chances. He was worried because of what happened when Caroline was pregnant with Kristen. He didn't want that to happen again.

Kristen and Steve made sure everything was cleaned in the house so Caroline wouldn't have any reason to do a thing. Kristen and Steve took turns making supper. They worked together every day to do dishes. Caroline became depressed because she couldn't do normal stuff anymore. Every morning, when Steve got to work, Roy would ask him how Caroline was doing. Steve told Roy she was getting restless and depressed. Roy and Catharine came over every weekend to see how Caroline was doing and to try to cheer her up.

It was now September 15. It was Saturday two weeks from Caroline's due date. Joseph and June came to visit. Caroline was upstairs lying down. Roy and Catharine came over later after lunch. Roy, Catharine, Joseph, and June were sitting on the couch talking. Kristen was in the kitchen helping Steve with the dishes. Suddenly, they heard Caroline scream. Steve told everybody to stay downstairs. He ran up to see what was wrong. When he got to the bedroom, Caroline was on her knees holding her stomach. Steve ran to her and said, "What's wrong, gorgeous? I heard you scream."

"Steve, something is wrong with the twins. I'm having bad cramping, and they are not labor pains. Oh god, I don't want to lose our twins, Steve," said Caroline.

"Honey, don't worry, you won't. Honey, can you try to walk downstairs?" asked Steve.

"No, it hurts too much," said Caroline.

Steve looked at Caroline who was getting pale. Her face showed she was in a lot of pain. He saw that Caroline started sweating. He felt her forehead, and it felt cold and clammy. He helped Caroline get back to the bed.

"Okay, gorgeous, stay here until I call for an ambulance," said Steve.

Steve ran down the stairs and everybody looked at him, wondering what was going on. He ran to the phone and called 911. When they heard him talking, they all knew something was seriously wrong with Caroline and the twins. Catharine, June, and Kristen ran upstairs to see Caroline. She was barely coherent.

"Mom, what's going on? Is it the twins?" asked Kristen. Caroline looked at Kristen and could barely hear her. Then blackness overtook her. Kristen looked at her mom lying so still. June yelled downstairs for Steve.

When Steve got done talking on the phone Roy and Joseph were standing right next to him. Steve's eyes showed fear in them.

"Dad, the ambulance is on its way. Something is wrong with the twins. Oh god, I don't want to lose Caroline or the twins," said Steve.

"Son, don't worry, you won't. Maybe they just want to come out early," said Joseph trying humorously to distract Steve.

"Telly, your dad is right. Maybe the twins don't want to be in the womb anymore. Maybe they're anxious to see their family. Don't worry until we know what's going on. We'll stay down here until the ambulance arrives so we can show them where to go. June just yelled for you. You better go up there. Caroline needs you," said Roy. Roy put his hand on Steve's shoulder to reassure him that Caroline would be okay.

Steve ran up to the bedroom. When he came into the room, he looked at Catharine, June, and Kristen who had tears in their eyes. He sat next to Caroline and grabbed her wrist to check for a pulse. Her pulse was very faint.

"Caroline, honey, hold on. The ambulance is on its way," said Steve.

He felt numb. His world was crumbling around him. He held Caroline's hand until the ambulance came.

When the ambulance got there. The paramedic immediately hooked Caroline up to a heart monitor. Putting her on a stretcher, they carried her to the ambulance. As the paramedics took Caroline out the front door, Steve looked at his mom and dad and at Roy and Catharine.

"Captain, can you call Mike and Janette and tell them what going on? Meet us at the hospital," said Steve.

The captain nodded his head and said, "Don't worry, Telly. I'll call Mike. Catharine, and I will see you at the hospital."

Steve looked at his mom and dad and said, "Mom and Dad, could you lock up for me and meet us at the hospital?"

"Son, just give me the keys. We'll see you at the hospital. We love you," said Joseph as he quickly hugged Steve and grabbed the keys out of Steve's hand.

Roy, Catharine, Joseph, June, and Kristen watched as the paramedics put Caroline in the ambulance. Steve jumped in after. After the ambulance left, Roy looked at Kristen and Catharine who were crying. He put his arms around her and Kristen and hugged them.

"Don't worry, Catharine, our girl will be just fine. She strong like Nathan and Kristy," said Roy.

"Roy is right. Caroline has been through worse things than this. It's just another obstacle she and Steve have to get through. Until we know what's going on, all of us need to be strong for Caroline, Steve, and the twins. Right now, they need our prayers and our support," said Joseph.

In the ambulance, the paramedics were working on Caroline. One of the baby's heartbeats started dropping. Steve kept looking at the heart monitor. He asked one of the paramedics what was wrong. The paramedic told him one of the babies might have the cord wrapped around its neck and that when they got to the hospital, they would have to do an emergency cesarean section to save the baby. When the paramedic said that, Steve's eyes widened. He looked painfully distressed and worried. The paramedic radioed ahead to let the hospital know they needed a doctor waiting for them. When they arrived at the hospital, the paramedics quickly got Caroline out of the ambulance and pushed her through the glass doors. Steve followed.

The doctor was waiting for them and started checking her vital signs. He looked at Steve and said, "We need you to sign some consent forms. I'll send a nurse out to bring the papers to you. I have to go now."

Steve just stood there dazed. He watched the doctor and the paramedics as they pushed Caroline down the hall. A nurse came up to him and handed Steve the papers to sign.

"Hi, my name is Judy. I'll be the one who will be helping you out until we find out what is going on. I work in the nursery. Your wife looks familiar," Judy said.

"Judy, is Caroline going to be okay?" asked Steve.

"She's in good hands. Your wife, was her name Caroline Winters?" asked Judy.

Steve looked at her and said, "Yes, her last name used to be that. Do you know my wife?"

"Yes, I've been taking care of the nursery for over eighteen years. I was here when she had Kristen our miracle baby," said Judy.

"Mr. Telly, don't worry and try to relax. You're not going to help Caroline by getting an ulcer. The doctor performing the operation has been through this before. He hasn't lost a baby yet. Follow me. I'll take you to the waiting room."

Steve felt more at ease at what Judy had just said. He followed Judy to the waiting room. "I'll see if I can find out how surgery is going. I'll be back. You really should try and relax," said Judy leaving the room.

Steve waited and waited. He started watching the clock. Twenty minutes later, Roy, Catharine, Joseph, June, and Kristen arrived at the hospital. They came directly to the emergency waiting room. When they walked into the waiting room, Steve was staring at the clock. They all sat down and looked at Steve. "I called Mitchell and Janette. Telly, what's wrong with Caroline?" asked Roy

"One of the baby's has the cord around its neck causing the heartbeat to drop. They're doing a cesarean section on Caroline. I haven't heard anything yet. I'm still waiting," said Steve.

Roy looked at how upset Steve was. He knew Steve was holding his feelings back. "Telly, let's go for a walk," said Roy.

They walked and talked. Roy tried to assure Steve that Caroline and the twins would be all right. At the same time, he was trying to assure himself. When Steve and Roy got back, they sat down and waited for the doctor.

Mike and Janette arrived a little later. They sat down across from Kristen and Steve. "Steve, have you heard how Caroline and the twins are?" asked Mike.

"No, we're still waiting," said Steve.

Ten minutes later, Judy, the nurse, came into the waiting room smiling. She felt the tension in the air when she entered the room. Everybody looked worried. She walked over to where Steve and Kristen were sitting. "Congratulations, I have good news for you. Mr. Telly, the surgery went very well. You were lucky you called 911 when you did. Otherwise, we might have had a different outcome. The twins are okay. The doctor checked them, and they are very healthy. Caroline is being taken to her room now. If you want, I'll take you to her room. She's going to be sleeping for a while until the anesthesia wears off. The doctor and I talked and thought it would be a good idea to bring the twins into Caroline's room so when she wakes up, the twins will be with her. So if everybody is ready," said Judy as she looked at everybody.

Before Judy got done talking, everybody was already standing ready to follow her smiling. Everybody followed Judy to Caroline's room. As they walked to the room, Judy looked at Kristen and said, "You must be Kristen, our miracle baby. You're so grown up now. I was hoping someday I would get to see you again. Your mom is a strong woman. She'll be okay."

When they got to the room, there was a nurse taking Caroline's vital signs. When she saw all the people coming into the room, she asked them how they were doing. She left the room to get more chairs so everybody could sit down. Judy went with the nurse to help carry the folding chairs. After Judy and the nurse brought the chairs in, they went to go get the twins.

Everybody waited, and Steve's dad started talking. "See, son, I told you the twins just wanted to meet our family early. They didn't want to wait two more weeks," said Joseph smiling.

"Yes, I guess you're right, Dad. But do you know what we forgot to ask Judy?" asked Steve.

"What son?" asked Joseph.

"We forgot to ask Judy whether the twins were boys or girls," said Steve.

Everybody realized Steve was right. Roy looked at Steve and said, "Telly, you're right. You being the daddy should've asked. Now we have to wait until they bring the twins in to find out," said Roy grinning.

"Captain, you're right, but it will be worth the wait, don't you think?" said Steve.

"You're right, Telly. It will be well worth the wait. I'll get to welcome my godchild into the world," said Roy.

When Judy and the other nurse brought the twins into the room, everybody watched. One baby had pink pj's on, and the other had blue. Everybody knew then that one was a girl and one was a boy. They all stood up to see the twins closer. The boy was bigger than the girl. Steve noticed his baby girl had a heart monitor hooked up to her. He looked at Judy and asked her a question, "Judy, why is my little girl hooked up to a heart monitor? Was she the baby whose heartbeat was dropping in the ambulance? Is she the one who had the cord around her throat?" asked Steve.

"Yes, the doctor is keeping it on her just to be safe. If your wife had the babies naturally, there would've been a good chance that your little girl wouldn't have survived. She would've been born first, but the way she was positioned with the cord around her throat would've cut the air supply off too long. The boy was already positioned where the little girl wouldn't have been able to turn herself around, so it's good that you and your family called 911," said Judy.

"When will Caroline wake up? Will it be soon?" asked Steve.

"The anesthesia should be wearing off soon," said Judy.

"Mr. Telly, you have such beautiful babies. Have you and Caroline talked about what you were going to name them?" asked Judy.

"Well, the boy we're going to name Jeffrey Steven Telly. The little girl is going to be named Hope Crystal Telly. Those were the only names we could come up with when the doctor told us she was going to have twins. We weren't sure what we were going to name the second twin if they would've been the same sex," said Steve.

"You and Caroline picked good names for them. I'm going to get back to the nursery. If you need anything, call me on my extension number. The babies are going to be with you until around seven PM, so you can spend time with Hope and Jeffrey and welcome them to the world." Roy and Catharine were standing by Hope Crystal admiring her. Mike and Janette were standing next to Jeffrey Steven, admiring him.

"We have the most beautiful grandchildren, don't we, June?" asked Joseph.

"Honey, our grandchildren are so precious. Kristen, what do you think? You have a brother and a sister," said June as she looked at Kristen.

"My brother and sister are so little and helpless right now. They'll need me to protect them from what they don't know, stuff that can hurt them. I can teach them a lot before I go to college. I can't wait until they can walk. They have such a loving, caring grandma and grandpa too," said Kristen. She hugged her grandparents. While everybody waited for Caroline to awaken, they took turns holding the babies. When Caroline awakened, Steve sat on her bed next to her. He kissed her and then hugged her.

"Well, gorgeous, would you like to meet the twins? Jeffrey Steven and Hope Crystal, meet your mommy," said Steve.

Roy and Catharine had Hope next to them. Roy carefully carried Hope to Caroline and put her in Caroline's arms. Then Mike carefully carried Jeffrey over to Caroline and handed him to Steve. Caroline was relieved that her twins were all right. She looked at Hope and then at Jeffrey.

"Steve, they're so perfect. I'm so glad they are all right," said Caroline.

Caroline looked at Roy and Catharine who were watching her. She looked down at Hope and then at Jeffrey. "Well, Hope Crystal, meet your godparents, Roy and Catharine Flynn," said Caroline smiling.

Roy and Catharine walked up to the bed, and Caroline handed Hope to them. Then she looked at Steve, who was holding Jeffrey. Steve knew what to do next. "Well Jeffrey Steven, meet your godparents, Mike and Janette Mitchell," he said, handing Jeffrey to Mike and Janette.

Steve and Caroline watched Roy, Catharine, Mike, and Janette with their godchildren. Joseph, June, and Kristen watched them also.

"Steven and Caroline, you've made them so happy by making them the godparents. Now everyone in this room is family. We all might not have the same blood, but all in all, we are one family. This is what family is all about. We all care about each other," said June smiling.

"Yes, Mom, you're right," said Steve.

June hugged Caroline and said, "I can't imagine what life would be like without my favorite and only daughter-in-law. We love you, Caroline."

After they finished talking, Roy brought Hope to June. He gently handed her to June and said, "Well, Hope, meet your grandma and grandpa. When you get older, your grandma and grandpa are going to spoil you and your brother, like me and Catharine."

As Roy said that, he winked at Joseph. Joseph stood there, grinning. Mike brought Jeffrey over to Joseph and handed him to Joseph. "Here you go, Grandpa, here is your grandson," said Mike. Mike looked like he was on cloud nine. Janette, Mike, Roy, and Catharine stood by Joseph and June, watching them.

Caroline hugged Kristen and Steve, and they watched everybody welcome the twins into the world. It was like Caroline and Kristen got a second chance to be happy again.

Roy, Catharine, Joseph, and June came to the hospital every day until Caroline and the twins could go home. Three days later, they were sent home. Steve and Roy picked Caroline and the twins up. Kristen, Mike, Janette, Joseph, Catharine, and June were waiting for them to bring her home with the twins. They were there to celebrate Caroline and the twins coming home. They had balloons everywhere you looked. The cake had a picture on it. It had two little babies on it. One was dressed in blue and the other in pink.

When they arrived, Caroline walked in first followed by Roy who had Hope in his arms and Steve who had Jeffrey in her arms. When she opened the door, everybody yelled, "Surprise!" And she turned around and looked at Steve and Roy who were smiling. When Steve came into the house, he looked at Caroline and said, "It was hard not to tell you what we were planning."

Steve carefully handed Jeffrey to Mike and walked over to Caroline and kissed her. Everybody went into the living room to visit and celebrate. Roy and Catharine went to visit their new family as much as they could. They didn't want to miss any special moments as the twins grew. Mike and Janette came over to visit as much as they could too. Every other weekend, Steve took Caroline, Kristen, and the twins to see his parents at their ranch.

Hope and Jeffrey grew fast. When they turned two months old, they were baptized. Their first words were *mama, dada, ampa, amma,* and *isten.*

Kristen helped her mom with the twins until they were a year old and then went to college. She decided to go to a college close to home. Every weekend, she came home to visit her parents and the twins. Occasionally Steve and Caroline would take Hope and Jeffrey to Kristen's dorm.

Life was finally good for this family who survived through hardships and tragedy.

To the reader, this is a fictional story. Many families have members who abuse alcohol and drugs. A number of teenagers drink and do drugs because of family problems or because their friends do it. They want to fit in with the crowd. Some teenagers can't resist the temptation of drugs and alcohol, and sometimes they abuse them. Often they get into predicaments similar to Kristen's. Some teenagers even die from alcohol and drug abuse. They are not as lucky as my character in the story. It is not always a happy ending in real life.

Ovarian cancer ranks second among gynecologic cancers. It causes more deaths than any other cancer of the female reproductive system. If it isn't caught early, the prognosis isn't good. In many cases, the woman doesn't survive.

ABOUT THE AUTHOR

She grew up in Wisconsin on a small farm.